Interview for a Wife

Nebraska Prairie Series, Volume 3

Ruth Ann Nordin

Published by Ruth Ann Nordin, 2022.

In loving memory of Wendell Nordin. (August 7, 1943 -July 15, 2021)

Thank you for helping me start on the path that led to me revisiting my love for writing. I wouldn't be where I am today if it hadn't been for your encouragement and support back in 2001. I'll see you when I get to Heaven.

Chapter One

LINCOLN, NEBRASKA

June 1880

The train pulled into the station. Deanne Grayson couldn't believe she was doing this. Who in their right mind would want to be interviewed in order to get married?

Someone who doesn't want to return to her parents' home.

Terry was dead, leaving her a widow. She had seen the advertisement from a man wanting a wife in the Omaha newspaper while packing to go back to live with her parents. She was about to dismiss it when she thought of how much she didn't want to return to Kentucky. If she could find a way to stay in Nebraska, why not do it?

The man who posted the ad was a widower with children. The ad said he needed a woman to assist him at the general store he owned and requested that she be a pleasant person who excelled at arithmetic. The ad ended by saying that if a woman was agreeable to such a business arrangement, he would be happy to interview her for the position.

It was a strange ad, now that she thought about it. At the time she'd decided to go, she hadn't given thought to the "business arrangement" part of the advertisement. She'd only thought she should at least go to Lincoln and meet him.

After convincing the owner of her apartment to let her keep her things there for one more week, she hopped the first train that would take her to Lincoln. And that brought her to where she was now. As the train came to a stop, Deanne renewed her grip on her travel bag.

Nothing ventured, nothing gained.

She'd left everything in Omaha, just in case things didn't work out. She took a deep breath and stood up after the conductor called out that it was safe to get off the train.

The station wasn't as big as the one in Omaha, which made it easier for her to find someone who could direct her to Harvey's General Store. After getting the directions, she left the station and headed down the boardwalk. Horse hooves clacked on the brick street as buggies and wagons passed along what had to be the business district of town.

She was glad to see there was a good selection of businesses to choose from. One thing she liked most about Omaha was the number of places to go. Her small Kentucky hometown hadn't had much to it, which was why she'd become a mail-order bride. No prospects were for her all the way back there, and while she no longer had the actual desire to be married again, she did want to do more than sit at home all day. She never wanted to go back to the restless feeling that had plagued her while growing up.

She went down several blocks before she came to the general store. She saw the sign on the window that read: *Wife Wanted: Apply Inside.* That was good. He hadn't found anyone to fill the position yet.

She opened the door, and the bell above it rang. She glanced up at it right before she heard someone coming out from the back. She turned her attention to a man with gray hair. He looked to be in his late sixties. Certainly, this couldn't be William Harvey.

"May I help you?" the man asked her.

She stepped further into the store and cleared her throat. "Yes, I'm here for the ad Mr. Harvey posted in the Omaha paper." She tried not to notice the way her voice echoed through the place. While there were a lot of items in the store, it was eerily devoid of people.

The man smiled. "I'll let him know you're here." He hurried to the back.

She shifted the travel bag from one hand to the other. Well, that particular man wasn't William Harvey. That was a relief. She hadn't really wanted to marry someone older than her father. But she did wonder what kind of man interviewed for a woman to marry him. Why not just place a mail-order bride ad like Terry had?

She heard the muffled sound of two men talking from the back room before the old man came back out. "Bill will see you," he told her.

"Bill?" she asked.

"That's what we call William Harvey around here. I'm Archie Smith. I'm helping him until he can get a wife to work in this store." He gestured for her to go with him to the back.

She hesitated to follow him. Couldn't Bill just come out here? She didn't know if she liked the idea of being alone with him, or with him and Archie, in a room in the back of this place.

The door behind her opened, and she turned in time to see a man, woman, and small child come into the store.

"I'll help them while you talk with Bill," Archie told her.

Feeling better about the situation, she nodded and went around the counter that led to the room. Now she didn't feel so vulnerable. If Bill did anything he shouldn't, all she had to do was cry out for help.

The room in the back was larger than she'd expected. It also had a window large enough to offer plenty of sunlight through the place. Half the room was full of excess items that couldn't fit into the main room of the store. A man who seemed to be in his mid-thirties sat behind a desk. He had dark wavy hair that reached just below his collar. He was clean-shaven, and he had a gentle expression on his face. She immediately felt better. He struck her as a respectable man, and he was only a few years older than her. Plus, he already had children. She might just manage alright in a marriage with someone like him.

"Archie didn't tell me your name," Bill said.

"My name is Deanne Grayson."

His eyebrows furrowed. "I don't recognize it. Are you new to Lincoln?"

"I'm from Omaha. I saw your advertisement in the paper."

"So, if I marry you, will you move to Lincoln? I'm in no position to leave this place."

"I'll move here. There's nothing keeping me in Omaha."

He gave her a nod. "Alright. Since that's the case, have a seat." He gestured to the chair across from his desk.

So far, so good. Ignoring the pounding of her heart, she pulled out the chair and sat down. She put the travel bag by her feet and clasped her hands in her lap. This wasn't much different from waiting for a response from the replies she'd sent out to men looking for a mail-order bride. The only difference was that she got a chance to see this particular man in person before he let her know whether or not he wished to marry her.

It didn't occur to her just how little choices women were granted until this moment. She had to hope he would pick her out of the other women he interviewed, just as she had to wait for the postmaster to bring her a letter from a man who would be her excuse to leave Kentucky.

She released her breath. She couldn't do anything about the way society was. All she could do was go along with it and pray this man wouldn't be like Terry.

"I put the questions I had written down somewhere on this desk," Bill said as he sorted through the papers scattered on it. "It's just my luck that you happened to arrive when I was in the middle of going through my receipts."

Since he smiled as he made the comment, she realized he was joking.

She relaxed. "If you tell me what the paper looks like, I can help you search for it," she offered, noting that he did have a lot of papers all over the place.

"It's one sheet, and I wrote on it with a pencil. I put the word *Interview* at the top." He stopped sorting through the papers in front of him and pointed to the edge of the desk. "There it is. Can you give that to me?"

She got up and retrieved it then held it out to him.

He thanked her and took it.

She returned to her chair and put her hands back on her lap. The paper had been closer to him than it'd been to her. She didn't know why he didn't stand up and grab it. She pushed the thought aside. It wasn't her place to question things. Maybe he was checking to see if she would be a helpful companion or not. The whole thing could have been a test. She was being interviewed after all.

He scanned the paper. "You'll have to forgive some of these questions. They'll be a bit personal, but I need to make sure the marriage will benefit both of us."

"I figured the questions would be personal since you're looking for a wife."

"Yes, well, it's still an unconventional way of doing things. A friend offered to match me up with someone, but I happen to know that the woman he has in mind wants children. The marriage would never work."

She leaned forward in interest. "But you have children, don't you?"

"I meant she wants children of her own. To answer your question, though, I have two of them. A girl and a boy. The girl is seven, and the boy is four. I had them with my first wife. She's no longer with us. Providence took her home two years ago."

"I'm sorry." Of course, she knew he was a widower. He'd mentioned that in the ad. But she was at a loss on what else she could say.

"I'm sorry, too, but I don't see any reason to dwell on things I can't change." He paused then added, "Most women want children of their own. I suppose there's no point in wasting our time. If you wish for children of your own, this arrangement won't work."

"No, I don't need to have children of my own." She decided not to tell him it was because she was unable to have any. He didn't need to know that. Though, the fact that it was even a concern to him made her curious about something. "You don't wish to have more children?"

"I'm happy with things as they are." His gaze went to the paper. "You appear to be in your late twenties. Is that correct?"

"I'm thirty-one."

"Thirty-one? Have you been married before?"

"Yes, but, like your wife, my husband is no longer living."

"Now I'm the one who's sorry."

He shouldn't be. She wasn't. But she bit her tongue on the thought.

"I take it that you and your husband lived in Omaha together?" he asked.

"Yes."

"Will there be anyone you'll miss if you move here?"

"No. My family is in Kentucky, but I have no desire to go back there."

"May I ask why?"

She wiped her hands on her skirt. What was the best way to word things? "I prefer to be appreciated for who I am rather than what I can do."

"That's understandable."

She held her breath, wondering if he would ask her more about her past, but fortunately, he changed the subject.

"A lot of this business involves being able to do arithmetic," he said. "Sometimes there's a line of customers, and it's important to be able to add and subtract accurately and quickly. The faster customers can get what they want and leave, the happier they are, though you have a couple who will talk all day if you let them." He chuckled. "Like Archie Smith. Ever since he had that grandson, he'll spend an hour bragging about him. But most people are busy and just want to be on their way. Some people put the amount on their account. In cases like that, I'll need you to tally up their debt until they come by to pay it off. A lot of them will pay you with cash, and they'll need change back. That's why I need someone who is quick with adding and subtracting."

"I can be quick," she replied. "Arithmetic was my favorite subject in school. I'm good at it, too. I rarely make an error."

"Mind if I test you?"

"No."

He paused for a moment then said, "A customer comes to you with items that cost $1.20, $0.05, $0.06, $0.25, and $0.35. What is the total cost they need to pay?"

"$1.91."

He blinked in surprise.

"I don't think I was wrong," she said.

"No, you're not wrong. It's just that I didn't expect you to give me the answer so fast." He paused. "Let's try another amount. $0.13, $0.24, $0.22, $0.12, and $0.08."

"$0.79."

She caught the way his lips curled up and knew she'd been right, once again.

"A box of matches is $0.50," he continued. "A pound of soap is $0.05. A pencil is $0.04. A pound of oatmeal is $0.04. A loaf of bread is $0.06."

"If a customer buys all of that, then they'll owe $0.69."

"What if they give you $0.75?"

"I'll give them $0.06 back."

"What if the customer gives you $1?"

"That one is too easy. It's $0.31."

She noted the amusement in his eyes. "Alright. A customer wants two pounds of salt which is $0.02 a pound, one pound of tea for $0.24, three pounds of cheese which is $0.13 a pound."

She took a moment before answering, "$0.67."

"I'm glad that one wasn't too easy," he said. "I was beginning to think you weren't human."

She chuckled. "I'm very human. I just love arithmetic."

"I can see that. It's an excellent quality, and it's one that I need. Can you read and write?"

"Yes, I can do that, too."

"Good because you'll need to mark down what you're selling and how much money you made in each transaction. I'll handle the other aspects of bookkeeping. You'll work out there." He pointed to the front of the store. "I'll work from here. Does that make sense?"

Her heart sped up. This had to mean he was going to give her the job. Or rather, marry her so she could do the job.

"There's only one more thing I need to get out of the way," he went on to say.

Noting the cautious tone in his voice, she straightened up. "What is it?"

"Since you've been married before, you're acquainted with the more intimate parts of a marital life."

Her eyebrows furrowed. Where could he be going with this? When she realized he expected her to say something, she replied, "Yes, I am."

He backed up from the desk but didn't stand up. Surprised, she rose to her feet to see how he had managed to do that. As soon as she saw that he was in a wheelchair, her face warmed, and she hurried to sit back down. She didn't know if her curiosity had just embarrassed him or not. She supposed it depended on how sensitive he was about being in a wheelchair. His pants were cut off and sewn just below the knees. Given that, there was no way he could walk.

He wheeled himself over to her. "I thought you should see why we won't be able to have the kind of intimacy we both had in our previous marriages."

By the way he said that, she knew he wasn't sure she'd be agreeable to the arrangement. He didn't know what her marriage had been like. He assumed it was a good one. Everyone assumed she'd been happy with her husband. And she had been, up until the time it became clear that she was barren and couldn't give him a child. After that, things were never the same between them.

"What I most want is someone whose company I can enjoy. I don't need the intimate moments in order to be happy," she said.

"I'd like companionship, too," he replied. "I miss having someone to talk to. I have friends and I have my children, but it's different being married to someone. There's something about marriage that brings you closer to a person than you can get with anyone else. You really do feel as if you're one with them."

She wouldn't know the feeling, but she smiled as if she did.

"You're the best lady who's come by to see me," he continued. "I think our marriage would be a good one. If you don't have any doubts about marrying me, I'd like for you to be my wife."

She wondered how many other women he had talked to, but she decided not to ask him about it. What did it matter? He had chosen her. That meant she could stay in Nebraska.

Since this was, thankfully, going to be a marriage where she wasn't going to be required to try to give him a child, she said, "I'd be happy to be your wife."

"Good." He smiled. "I can take care of the arrangements for the wedding. Given my situation, I prefer something small and informal. Will that bother you?"

"No, I don't mind small and informal." She had no one she was bringing to the wedding anyway. Like the first one, she would be by herself. "I will need to return to Omaha to collect my things, but everything can fit in one trunk."

His gaze went to the travel bag by her feet. "Are you returning there today?"

"No, I have a ticket for tomorrow. I wasn't sure if I was going to be interviewed right away, so I thought it best to stay overnight. I was planning to find an inn after this."

"I can't have you stay at an inn. I'd offer you a room at my house, but people would assume the worst and I want to protect your reputation."

That was understandable, especially in light of the fact that she'd be working in this store. People needed to feel comfortable doing business with her.

"I'm sure Henry and Marsha Willard will see to your accommodations tonight," he said as he wheeled himself over to the door separating this room from the main part of the store.

She rose to her feet and followed him. "I can't impose. I have enough money to stay at an inn. My husband had some money saved." It wasn't enough to let her live in Nebraska for the rest of her life, but it was sufficient for a few months.

"It's not an imposition," Bill replied. "Henry and Marsha are my uncle and aunt. They offered to help my new wife in any way they could. When you marry me, they'll be a part of your family. Also, they're taking care of Amber and Vernon. Those are my children. They stay with them while I'm here at the general store. My wife used to watch them while I was here. After she died, Marsha volunteered to watch them for me during the day. They come home with me at night. It will probably be good if you meet them."

Up to now, her main concern had been whether or not she'd get to stay in Nebraska. Now a wave of apprehension washed over her. She'd had so little interaction with children. She didn't know what to do with them. She supposed they should be treated like anyone else, except they were bound to need proper moral instruction given their age.

"Will they mind that I'm going to be taking over the role of their mother?" Deanne asked.

"I don't think so. I do my best to do the job of two parents, but I don't have the soft touch a woman does. I held off on another marriage because I wasn't ready to be with someone right after losing Jennifer, but I'm ready now. I think the children will like having you around. I don't foresee there being any problems."

She took a deep breath and slowly released it. The reassuring tone in his voice helped to soothe her nerves. "Alright. I'll be happy to stay with your aunt and uncle, and I'll do my best to give your children the care and nurture they need."

"You might as well think of them as your children. As far as I'm concerned, once we marry, that's what they'll be."

Yes, she supposed he was right. And that actually came as a relief. People would stop giving her pitying looks or ask why she didn't have any children. The fact that Bill had children was going to save her a lot of grief.

"I'll tell Archie we're leaving, and then I'll take you to Henry and Marsha's," he said.

She almost asked him if he wanted her to push his wheelchair, but he wheeled himself into the main part of the store before she could say anything. Her cheeks warmed from embarrassment. She must not think of him as an invalid. She didn't like it when people thought something was wrong with her for not being able to have children. That being the case, she wouldn't think he was less of a person because he was in a wheelchair.

She hurried to retrieve her travel bag then followed him.

Chapter Two

SEVEN-YEAR-OLD AMBER and four-year-old Vernon came running over to Bill as soon as he and Deanne arrived at his aunt and uncle's house.

"You're early," Amber said as she and Vernon hugged him. "Is it time to go home?"

"No, not yet." Bill gestured to Deanne who stood nearby with the travel bag in hand. "Do you remember what I said about looking for a wife to help me out at the store?"

Vernon shook his head, but Amber nodded.

Bill chuckled and told Deanne, "Vernon's young. He doesn't remember everything I tell him." His gaze went to the boy. "The woman I'm going to marry will not only help me with the store, but she'll help me take care of you two as well. She's going to be your new mother. Her name is Deanne, but I want you to call her 'Ma.'"

Amber indicated she would do as he wished, but Vernon just stared at Deanne as if he'd never seen a woman before.

Deanne offered a smile that indicated she wasn't sure what she should say to them.

"I know it's going to take everyone time to adjust to all of this," Bill said. "We'll just take things one day at a time." Turning his attention to his children, he added, "She'll stay here tonight with Uncle Henry and Aunt Marsha. Then she'll return to Omaha to pack so she can come here to be with us permanently."

Amber opened her mouth to respond, but Aunt Marsha opened the front door and called out, "What are you doing here so early, Bill?"

"I found a woman to marry," he replied. "Deanne Grayson came all the way from Omaha to answer my ad. She's exactly what I've been looking for. I thought you might let her stay here for the night."

"I won't be any trouble," Deanne told her. "I have a ticket to return to Omaha tomorrow."

"Oh, I know you won't be any trouble," his aunt said. "Henry and I will be happy to have you as our guest. I'll take that travel bag for you. You can have our daughter's bedroom."

Bill caught the worried expression on Deanne's face and assured her, "Stephanie doesn't live here anymore. She lives in Grand Island with her husband."

The answer seemed to satisfy her since he saw her relax. She handed the travel bag to his aunt.

"I better get back to work," Bill said. "I have a lot of receipts to go through, but I should be here for dinner on time."

His aunt gave him a nod. "That sounds good, Bill. We'll have dinner when you get here." She gestured for the children to go into the house then started telling Deanne about the menu she had planned for the evening.

Deanne gave him a quick glance before she went into the house with his aunt and children. Maybe he should have kept her at the store longer. The poor woman must feel all alone out here where she was far from any family and friends.

She might have had a husband before and she might be surprisingly gifted at arithmetic, but this new life was bound to take her time to get used to. All he could do was be there to help her as much as the wheelchair allowed. With a sigh, he turned the wheelchair around and headed back to the general store.

DEANNE TRIED NOT TO be self-conscious as Amber and Vernon stared at her, but it became more and more difficult as the afternoon wore on. No matter what she did or what room she was in, they just watched her. The only time they said anything was when Marsha asked them a question. Had Marsha not been with her, Deanne might have bolted out of the house after the first hour passed.

She had no idea that children were so curious. But she'd rather go through a million afternoons of awkwardness than return to Kentucky. She'd endured far worse than this.

She took another glance at the children who sat across from her at the table while she cut the vegetables for the salad Marsha was making.

"Are you going to be a good ma?" Amber asked her.

Deanne blinked in surprise. It was the first time Amber spoke directly to her. She offered the girl what she hoped was a reassuring smile. "I'm going to be the best ma for you and your brother than I can be."

Amber's eyebrows furrowed. "Does that mean you'll be good?"

She thought the answer was obvious, but perhaps it wasn't to a young child. "Yes, I will be good."

"Have you been a ma before?"

"No, I'm sorry to say I haven't."

Amber looked over at her brother who just kept his eyes focused on Deanne. Deanne couldn't be sure, but she didn't think the boy had blinked in over a minute.

"The ma I used to have was good," Amber said.

"I'm sure she was," Deanne replied.

"Vernon doesn't remember her. He was a baby when she died."

"I'm sorry."

Vernon finally blinked, but he still kept his attention on Deanne.

Forcing aside her unease, Deanne picked up a carrot and cut it. "No child should lose their mother."

"She was wearing a green dress the day she died," Amber said. "Pa took me to the hospital to see her. I don't remember anything else from that day. But I remember her singing to me."

"I bet she was a nice person."

"She was. I miss her."

Deanne thought over how she should reply, and after a moment, she settled for saying, "I don't intend to replace her. I know I'll never be the mother she was. All I can promise is that I will think of you and your brother as my own children."

"If you haven't been a ma before, how do you know how to treat children?"

The girl didn't come up with questions that were easy to answer. She wondered if Bill had any idea how smart his daughter was.

Fortunately, Marsha said, "Women have a natural mothering instinct about them, Amber. You have no need to worry about your new ma. She'll be nice to you and your brother."

The answer seemed to satisfy the girl since she nodded in approval. Then, to Deanne's surprise, she asked Marsha, "Does that mean I'll be a good ma?"

Marsha smiled. "You're already a good sister. That mothering instinct is already right in here." She tapped the girl's heart. "It's not how long someone has been a mother that matters. What matters is what's in her heart. Your pa wouldn't have picked someone who wouldn't be good to you and your brother." She turned her kind gaze to Deanne. "If you have any questions about Amber or Vernon, don't hesitate to ask. I've known them since the day they were born."

"Was Ma happy when we were born?" Amber asked her.

"She was very happy. Your pa was, too," Marsha replied.

Deanne had no doubt about that. She recalled the tenderness in Bill's voice when he spoke about his children. She was sure he was just as concerned that he could give them a good mother as he was about finding a qualified person to help him manage the store. What was it about her he saw that prompted him to pick her when he could have picked someone else? Surely, she couldn't be the only woman who could do basic arithmetic in her head.

"My husband will come home with Bill in about an hour," Marsha told Deanne. "He'll take them home after dinner."

Deanne's eyebrows furrowed. "Bill doesn't live in town?"

"He lives a few miles outside of town," Marsha said. "He wants to move into town, but he can't get anyone to buy the small farm he currently lives on. His first wife inherited it from her parents. They came out here on a wagon train. All of her other relatives are back East. None of them want to live out here."

Deanne had heard of wagon trains but couldn't imagine ever traveling so far on foot. "Her parents must have been brave people."

"It's not as dangerous on the wagon trains as some would have you believe, but trains are a more efficient way to go from one place to another," Marsha said.

"I'm glad for them," Deanne replied.

"Are trains fun to ride?" Amber asked her.

"I wouldn't say they're fun," Deanne began, "but they are affordable and faster than going on a horse or on foot."

"Until we have a better way of transportation, people will keep using them," Marsha told the girl. "Now, why don't you take your brother out to the backyard to play while your ma and I finish making dinner?"

"Alright." Amber took her brother by the hand and led him out the door that led to the yard.

Marsha chuckled. "Every child stares at a stranger, and once they're done staring, they ask questions. They're just curious."

Deanne's face warmed. Had the woman noticed how apprehensive she felt around Amber and Vernon? She smiled, hoping she hadn't given away her unease. "I'm sure I'll get used to being a mother soon enough."

"You will." Marsha patted her shoulder. "It'll come to you. You'll be surprised at how fast you'll adjust to motherhood."

Deanne could only hope the woman was right.

Chapter Three

AUNT MARSHA AND UNCLE Henry did most of the talking at dinner. Bill did what he could to add to the discussion, but he'd heard the stories they were telling Deanne and the children a dozen times already. He could practically recite them word for word.

What he most wanted to do was speak with Deanne in private. He didn't get a chance to do that, though, because she volunteered to help his aunt do the dishes. He managed to resist the urge to tell her she didn't need to help wash the dishes because he could tell it was important to her that she earn her keep. She didn't want things just handed to her. He could respect that. In fact, it was an admirable trait. So he joined his uncle in sitting on the front porch and watched the children play in the yard.

The day had been a good one. Despite the amount of receipts he'd had to go through a second time because he found some in another pile on his desk after he thought he was all done recording them into his ledger, he did find the right woman to marry. He was beginning to worry he'd never find someone. Out of the six who had come to see him, five had wanted children of their own. There was one who was fine with the idea they'd never consummate the union. Then she blanched when she realized he was bound to a wheelchair, and he knew it would never work.

Deanne, thankfully, hadn't been appalled by the fact that he was only half a man. There had been the flicker of surprise on her face, but it'd been quickly replaced with acceptance. It was then he knew the match would be a suitable one. It probably wasn't going to lead to love, but he thought they might form a comfortable companionship.

"I think you picked a good woman to marry," Uncle Henry said.

Bill took his attention off of Amber and Vernon so he could look at him.

Uncle Henry chuckled. "Your aunt told me Amber asked Deanne if she was going to be a good mother. Your aunt said that Amber isn't sure if a woman who's never been a mother before knows what to do."

Bill smiled. "Amber was born a worrier. I think that's why God let her be born first. That way she can look after her little brother."

"She is a mother hen. I think she wouldn't know what to do with her time if she didn't have Vernon."

"She'd find something to watch over."

"She's a sweet girl."

"Yes, she is." She reminded him a lot of Jennifer, and it comforted him to see that a part of Jennifer was going to live on in their daughter.

"Amber and Vernon will get used to Deanne," his uncle said. "It'll take some time, but they'll adjust. Children are good about accepting changes. And, of course, your aunt and I will treat Deanne as part of the family."

"I don't think there will be any problems. Deanne has the same gentle look about her that Jennifer did. I'm glad she came. I was beginning to give up hope I was going to find someone."

"The Lord answers prayers. Sometimes you just need to be patient. I'm sure Archie will be glad to get back to spending his days on the farm with his daughter and son-in-law and their newborn son."

Bill gave his uncle an amused look. "Would you believe Archie's grandson is almost six months old?"

"Already?"

"Yep."

"It's not right that little ones grow up so fast. It's enough to make someone like me feel old."

"You're plenty young. You haul supplies all over town. As long as you can keep lifting heavy things, you're young."

"I won't be young much longer if these little ones get to be adults." Bill chuckled.

The front door opened, and he saw his aunt looking at them in surprise. "What are you still doing here? I thought Henry was going to take you three home right after dinner."

"I want to talk to Deanne about the preacher," Bill replied.

"Why didn't you say so? I would have made Henry help me with the dishes." She gestured for Henry to go to the carriage house. "Go on and get the wagon ready so Bill and Deanne can talk alone."

Henry rolled his eyes but was grinning as he left the porch.

"I'll tell her to come out," Marsha told Bill before she slipped back into the house.

Bill glanced at the children. They were still playing, though poor Vernon was already yawning. Bill could only hope he could keep the boy awake until they got home. If the boy fell asleep on the way home, it would take forever to get him to settle into bed for the night.

Deanne came onto the porch and hurried to sit next to him. "I'm sorry. I didn't realize you wished to have a word with me. I thought you and the children already left."

"It's alright. I just wanted to let you know that I spoke with the preacher. He said he'll marry us when you return. I don't know how much time you need in order to get your things ready."

"I was supposed to move out of my apartment two days ago, but the owner gave me an extra week."

"In that case, it sounds like it'd be best if you move here as soon as possible."

"To be honest, it would. I can have everything done and be here in three days. I saw your ad while I was packing. I was ready to return to my family in Kentucky, but I'd much rather stay in Nebraska. I love it out here."

"I'm glad to hear that because I love it out here, too." He gave her a smile. "I won't lie. It'll be nice to have your help."

"I'll do anything I can."

He didn't doubt it. After talking to her at the store and seeing how she was around his family, he knew he was getting a good deal in this marriage. "When you come back, I'll arrange for someone to get your trunk and have it delivered to my store. Henry can bring it to my house, but don't be in a rush to unpack everything. I'm hoping to move into town before the year is up. Being in a wheelchair makes the tasks on the farm too difficult to manage. And that's even after I sold the animals."

"I'm sure you also want to live close to the store. I imagine you spend a lot of time there."

"Sometimes I'm there for ten or twelve hours. It just depends on how far behind I get in the recordkeeping."

"I hope I can help lessen your time on that. I don't mean to brag, but I can do more than add and subtract numbers in my head."

"I look forward to finding out how much you'll surprise me," he said.

"Vernon's sleeping!" Amber called out as she ran over to them.

Bill looked over at his son who had fallen asleep in the grass. He sighed. "I better get home."

"I'll let your uncle and aunt know you're ready to go." Deanne stood up, gave Amber a smile that clued Bill in on how uncertain she was about her ability to be a mother, and went into the house.

"Pa, can't we stay here tonight?" Amber asked. "I'm tired, too."

"Aunt Marsha and Uncle Henry don't have room for all of us," he replied. "We'll be home soon."

His uncle pulled the wagon up to the house.

"See?" Bill gave her arm a pat. "Get your doll."

As she ran to the house, he wheeled himself down the ramp. He was relieved Deanne would return within a few days. Archie would be happy about it, too. The poor man had done so much to help him, but he should be on his farm to help his daughter and her family.

His heart lighter than it'd been in quite some time, he went to the wagon while his uncle lifted a sleepy Vernon from the grass.

TWO DAYS LATER, DEANNE was in the process of making sure she wasn't going to leave anything in her apartment when a knock came at her door. The person turned out to be the wife of the man who owned the apartment building.

"How are you, Mrs. King?" she asked the woman. "I was about to go downstairs to tell you that I'll be leaving tomorrow morning. Everything is packed and ready to go."

"Oh, I didn't come here to pester you about moving out again," the woman replied. "I came to bring you this letter. I didn't want you to forget to check your box, so I took the liberty of checking it for you."

"Thank you." Forcing the smile to stay on her face, Deanne accepted it from her. One thing she wasn't going to miss was the woman's habit of snooping into her business.

"I hope you don't mind, but I couldn't help noticing it's from Alonzo and Betsy Cooper who are in Kentucky. You came from Kentucky. Are they your parents?"

"Yes," she reluctantly answered. This was her last day in this apartment. She could manage to be pleasant for one more day.

"You never mentioned your parents," the woman said. "I assumed they were dead."

"Oh, well, I'm a private person. I don't say much of anything to anyone."

"Yes, that's very true. It's unfortunate. We could have gotten to know each other better. You missed a lot by not coming to my casual get-togethers with some of the other ladies in this apartment."

Deanne hated it whenever she brought up the afternoons when she and the other busybodies in the apartment got together. Deanne suspected the coffee and card games were just an excuse to gossip. She had heard whispers of what those women had said about her and Terry over the years, especially when Terry visited Malorie a little too often and Malorie had the child that looked too much like him.

Hoping it would be enough to make the landlady go away, Deanne hugged her and said, "Thank you for all of the kindness you've shown me and Terry over the years."

Thankfully, that did the trick. The woman smiled and patted her back. "I hope things go well for you in Lincoln."

"It seems like it will. I'm looking forward to working." Deanne had opted not to tell the woman about Bill or the fact that she was getting married. All she'd said was that she got a job in Lincoln.

"Sometimes the thing an aching heart needs is a purpose."

"Yes, I agree, and this will give me a wonderful purpose."

"Before you leave tomorrow, will you tell me? I want to know when I can put up an advertisement for the apartment."

"I'll let you know."

Finally, mercifully, the woman left, and Deanne was able to return to her world of peace.

Chapter Four

"YOUR BRIDE JUST GOT off the train," Archie said as he bounded into the back room where Bill was filing the receipts he'd just recorded for yesterday's purchases.

"Is she here?" Bill asked.

"Not yet. I just got word from Preacher Thompson's wife that they're bringing Deanne's trunk over," Archie replied. "It sounds like Deanne is still at the train station."

Bill's eyebrows furrowed. "She didn't run into any trouble, did she?"

He shrugged. "No one said anything was wrong."

Bill slipped the folder into the drawer then backed up from his desk and wheeled out of the back room. "Will you keep watch over the place while I go to the station and make sure everything's alright?"

"Will do." Archie went back behind the counter.

Bill greeted a couple of the patrons who were shopping in the store as he left.

At times, it frustrated him to no end that going anywhere in the wheelchair was much slower than walking. And even more frustrating was the fact that he couldn't go directly into the train station since there were no ramps. He had to ask a boy who had nothing better to do than sit on a step and eat candy if he'd go into the station and find Deanne for him.

The boy went in, and soon, Deanne came out with the boy. Her gaze locked with Bill's, and she hurried down the steps.

"Is something wrong?" Bill asked her.

"I can't find my purse," she replied. "The string broke, and it must have rolled under the seats."

"Did you have anything important in it?"

"Just some money, a pocket watch, and a letter. There's nothing in there I absolutely need."

"Well, don't worry about the money. I have enough to take care of things. As for a pocket watch, we can get that for you later."

She glanced back at the train station and sighed. She probably realized, just as much as he did, that there wasn't going to be sufficient time to find it before the train left, especially with people getting settled into their seats.

"Is the letter important? We can ask the station manager to have someone search for the purse and send a note to the store if it's found."

She hesitated. "No, I don't care about the letter."

"Then everything will be fine," he assured her. "As long as there's nothing you absolutely need, then you might as well let it go."

"Yes, I suppose so." After a moment, she relaxed. "What a way to start our marriage, huh?"

He chuckled. "If this is the worst of it, we'll do just fine. Since your trunk is being taken to the store, we might as well go to the preacher's. Then I'll take you to my aunt and uncle's. You can start work tomorrow."

"Please let me start work today."

Surprised, he asked, "You want to work today?"

"I've been looking forward to using my arithmetic skills. I haven't had a chance to apply myself to anything that really matters in years. I want to help out."

He was sure she had been useful to her first husband, but she probably felt like she'd had no purpose after he died. Bill struggled for the longest time to feel like his life had any meaning after Jennifer died, and having the store to run helped a lot in that regard.

"Alright," he agreed. "We'll go to the store after we get married."

Noting her relief, he told her which way they needed to go and started wheeling his chair in the direction of the preacher's house.

"THE LEDGER IS RIGHT here," Archie was telling Deanne an hour later after she and Bill married. "You write the items that were purchased, the total, and whether someone paid cash or will pay later on here. Sometimes the orders get to be big. The people who don't live in town like to get enough to see them through for a few months. So in that case, I list everything on a piece of paper from this stack over here." He patted the blank sheets of paper that were next to a couple of pencils.

"You just need to tuck the paper into the ledger when we close the store," Bill told her. "I'll file it away the next day."

"That sounds simple enough," she replied as she mentally made a note of everything they were telling her.

"It is," Archie said. "Unless you have a few customers at once. Then it can get complicated."

"If you get overwhelmed, ring the bell, and I'll come out and help," Bill added.

She saw the small bell next to the candy on the counter. Oh. So the bell wasn't for sale. It was such a cute thing she thought it might be a toy for a child.

"It might be best to put the bell by the ledger and papers," Bill told Archie.

"Good idea." Archie hurried to move it.

She felt a smile tug at her lips. If she guessed right, the two men got along very well. Being with them made her feel at ease. It'd been a long time she'd felt that way around anyone.

The door opened, and a couple who appeared to be in their early twenties entered the store. A young child was holding the woman's hand.

"That's Pete and Ada Kelly, and that's their boy, Fred. Ada's a good friend of my daughter's," Archie whispered to Deanne. "Now, Pete doesn't hear, so we have to use our hands to talk to him. I only know a few words. Thankfully, Ada helps me by signing to him." He drew away from Deanne and waved to the couple. "How's it going today?"

"We're doing fine," Ada replied. Letting go of Fred's hand, she made gestures with her hands while she continued, "We came for some fabrics and buttons. Fred needs new clothes already."

"That's impossible," Archie said in surprise. "Didn't you just make that boy some new pants and shirts?"

Ada signed to her husband before answering Archie, "Yes, but Fred's already too big for them. See?" She bent down and showed them the hem of the pants which was above his ankle.

"It's not fair they grow up so fast," Archie told Deanne and Bill.

Bill indicated his agreement then told Ada, "You're in luck. We just got a new shipment of fabrics in the other day." He pointed around the corner. "They're over there. Before you go, though, I want to introduce you to my wife, Deanne. We just got married."

"Yeah, so you'll be seeing her pretty face around here instead of my old one," Archie added.

The group laughed at his joke before Deanne offered a greeting. Ada returned the greeting then moved her hands so fast that Deanne couldn't even fathom what she was signing to Pete. Pete, in turn, signed back just as fast. After a moment, Fred joined in.

Deanne took a deep breath and turned her attention to the ledger. If she had to keep watching that, she might get dizzy. She couldn't imagine she'd ever be that fast with signing if she had to do that. She supposed she better learn some of the basic words to sign since Pete was going to be one of the customers she'd need to assist.

"We can help Pete and Ada with this purchase," Archie told Bill. "I'll show Deanne how we calculate the fabrics."

Bill glanced her way. "Do you feel comfortable out here without me?"

Despite her apprehension, she assured him she'd be just fine. She had to get used to this job sometime, and now was as good a time as any.

As he wheeled himself to the back room, she followed Archie and Ada to where the fabrics were.

AFTER DEANNE HELPED Bill close the store, Henry came over with another man, and they put her trunk on the back of Henry's wagon. She ate dinner with Bill, his children, and his aunt and uncle. She mostly listened as they talked.

She never was good around a lot of people, and though one might think it was silly, she considered any group larger than two to be a lot of people. They seemed happy since they did a lot of laughing and talking. They were talking so fast that she could hardly keep up with the conversation. She hoped they didn't think she was boring. Or worse, she hoped they didn't end up deciding they didn't like her.

The ride in the wagon out of town was surprisingly much more subdued than dinner had been. Amber spent the majority of the thirty-minute ride singing a song she'd learned earlier that day. Deanne didn't mind. She was just glad that listening to Amber and telling the girl she enjoyed the song was enough to please her.

It turned out the fields and fenced-in-pasture of the farm went untouched. At one time, this farm had probably had a lot of animals and crops on it. She had no idea how long it'd been since anyone tended to the land out here, and she didn't feel it was her place to ask. All Bill had told her was that he was selling it so he could move to town Considering everything, that was the best decision. She'd do the same in his position.

Henry helped her down from the wagon. She turned to help the children down, but they jumped down from it and ran for the barn before she could blink.

"They like to check the cats," Bill said as Henry set the wheelchair on the board walkway that led to the ramp that went to the porch. "The cats take care of the mice. They're useful to have out here." Henry put an arm under Bill's thighs and another under Bill's arms before he helped him down from the wagon.

Deanne turned her gaze away. She probably shouldn't worry about being caught staring at them, but she wasn't sure if she was allowed to watch this part of things. If she'd been around someone who had been in a wheelchair or who had to deal with some other physical condition in the past, she might know how to act. Unfortunately, unless she was using math around Bill, she couldn't completely relax. The work at the store was safe. It gave her something tangible to focus on. This whole thing of being his wife outside of the store was going to take some time to get used to.

If Bill noticed her uncertainty, he didn't show it. He unlocked the wheels and said, "Ladies first."

Her cheeks warm, she hurried up the ramp, thinking too late that there was no way he could catch up to her. She would have probably been better off going at a slower pace. She hoped she didn't make him feel self-conscious about not being able to move as fast as she could.

She turned and waited for him as he made his way up the ramp.

When he reached her, he gestured to the door. "It's not locked. You can go in."

"Oh." She went to the door and opened it.

"I don't know if you have to lock doors in Omaha, but out here, you don't. It's a quiet community. We all take care of each other. The poor sheriff has little to do. I think the biggest excitement he's had all month is helping one of the ladies in town get a cat down from a tree."

She relaxed at his easy-going manner.

He wheeled himself into the house, and after a quick debate, she followed him.

"Henry will bring your trunk in," Bill said. "Your bedroom will be upstairs. It's the biggest one up there. It's the second one on the right. Amber and Vernon sleep up there, too, but they're in a different room. I sleep down here on the couch."

She glanced in the room closest to them and saw the blanket and pillow that had been neatly placed on the couch. A dresser had been set up across the room. The chairs and table one usually found in a parlor had been removed so he could have plenty of space to move around in the wheelchair.

"There is a bedroom by the kitchen," he continued, "but it's easier to move this chair around this room. I'm using that other room as a parlor. If you want to have any women to come and visit, you can visit there."

She doubted she'd have friends, but she chose not to say anything. He didn't have to know how socially inept she was. He had married her because she was good with adding and subtracting. He didn't marry her so she could entertain visitors. At least she didn't think that would be part of the arrangement.

"Do you want me to entertain guests in our home?" she asked.

"Whether or not you want to do that is up to you," he replied. "My main concern is how you'll be with the children and how well you can handle the job at the store."

She relaxed. Good. She hadn't misunderstood him. She smiled. "I can handle those things, though it'll probably take me time to adjust to being a mother."

He smiled in return. "It took me time to adjust to being a father. When you first hold a little one and realize you're responsible for them, it scares you. No one is born knowing how to be a parent. It's just something that comes from the heart."

She hoped her heart would tell her what to do because the thought of being a mother still frightened her. She took a deep breath and exhaled it. "Do you mind if I check out the rest of the house?"

"Please do. I'd go with you, but I think I'll only slow you down. The wheelchair doesn't work so well through most of the rooms. The only places I can easily go to are the kitchen and the room where I sleep."

The poor man. She couldn't imagine being so limited in where she could go. She'd taken the ability to walk for granted.

"Do you want a glass of water or something?" she asked. "I can bring something back after I find the kitchen."

"I'll get it later. Go on and make yourself at home."

He wheeled himself into the room he was using as a bedroom. Taking that as her cue, she turned down the hall and checked the little room that he had converted into a parlor. The chairs were close together, and there was a table in the middle of the room. It had curtains that were just as pretty as the ones in the room he was sleeping in. She went to the kitchen and found that the same type of curtains were in there, too. She even saw other things that his first wife had brought into the home. There was a pretty cabinet with china dishes. The walls had been painted a pleasant peach color. There were even cute little animals that had been painted along the walls.

He had kept the things his first wife had added to this home. It was sweet that he had cared so much for her that he didn't get rid of her things. She experienced a slight twinge of jealousy, but she forced it down. Her first husband hadn't cared one way or another about her. She hadn't married him knowing if he would love her or not, but toward the end, he had so much contempt for her that she was happy to throw out everything that reminded her of him. The last thing she ever wanted to do was remember Terry.

She took a moment to calm her emotions before she checked out the mudroom and then went up the stairs.

She made it to the second bedroom just as the door opened downstairs. She heard the excited children tell Bill about the cats. Then she heard Henry call out that he had her trunk.

She returned to the top of the stairs and yelled out, "I'm up here!"

Amber ran up the stairs ahead of him, but Vernon trailed after.

When Amber reached her, she said, "I'll tell you where you can put the trunk."

Surprised the girl assumed she didn't know where to put a trunk, Deanne followed her into the larger of the two rooms.

"There's a spot right here," Amber said, pointing to a vacant place in the corner.

There wasn't much to the room. The bed was made with a couple of pillows and clean bedding. There was a dresser with a large mirror above it and a basin with a washbowl. A neatly folded washcloth and bar of soap was next to the basin. Other than that, it was bare. Though it did have nice decorative curtains.

Henry came into the room.

"The trunk can go here," Amber said.

He glanced at Deanne to make sure that was alright. When Deanne nodded, he put the trunk down in that spot. "I'll take this pitcher and fill it with water," he told Deanne as he retrieved it.

"The water from the well is cold," Amber said after he left the room.

"Cold water doesn't bother me," Deanne replied.

"I hate it. I like to wait until I get to Aunt Marsha's to wash up. She heats water up for me," the girl said. "Vernon likes the warm water, too."

Deanne glanced at the boy as he climbed onto her trunk. She wasn't sure what he planned to do with it until he jumped up and down on it.

"Vernon, that's not nice," Amber admonished, putting her hands on her hips. "This is a nice trunk. You don't want to ruin it."

"It's fun," Vernon replied as he continued jumping.

Amber rolled her eyes. "Kids. What are you going to do?" She went to the trunk and pointed to the floor. "Get down right now!"

Vernon grew stiff and then hurried to obey.

"It's time to get to bed," Amber told her brother. "Come on. I'll help you."

As Amber and Vernon left her bedroom, Deanne wondered if she should be the one making sure Vernon got ready for bed. She was their mother now. Surely, making sure children got ready for bed was a mother's job. Wasn't it?

Henry returned to her room with the pitcher of water and an empty glass. "This should see you through the night and morning. I usually take care of Amber and Vernon, so I'll do that tonight. Then you can start on that tomorrow. I'll be here at 6:30. Bill and I made sure there's plenty of food in the kitchen for you to make breakfast. Bill and the kids used to come out to my place to eat breakfast, but Bill thought you'd rather cook here in the mornings."

"Yes, I would." While she was relieved she didn't have to go through the trouble of figuring out how to get children ready for bed tonight, she did want to do everything that was expected of her tomorrow.

Henry wished her a good night and went to the next room. She listened to him and the children while she put her things away. It took a while to realize he was telling them a story. Amber asked a lot of questions about it, but Vernon remained quiet.

As she put her brush and pins out on the dresser, Deanne's exhaustion caught up to her, and she found herself yawning. What a day it'd been.

But she'd made it to Lincoln. That was what mattered. Though she'd lost her purse, it could have been worse. She'd much rather be in this house with Bill and his children than on her way back to Kentucky. At least here, she might be happy. And if not happy, then content.

She closed her bedroom door so she could get ready for bed. Once she was in her nightgown, she slipped under the covers.

She heard Henry go downstairs and say something to Bill. Then the front door shut, and he took the wagon to his home.

Her eyelids drooped, and she felt sleep sneaking up on her. She had gone through enough for one day. Tomorrow would take care of itself. She closed her eyes, and before long, she was fast asleep.

Chapter Five

DEANNE WOKE UP THE next morning right before the sun rose. She washed up and got dressed in the faint light of the moon. If she had thought about it, she would have asked for a candle or a kerosene lamp.

By the time she was brushing her hair, the sun was finally rising for the day, and it gave her enough light to see what she was doing as she pinned her hair up.

She had no way of knowing what time it was. She used to own a pocket watch, but that had been in her purse. After slipping her boots on, she left the room. She stopped in front of the other bedroom and opened the door a crack. The children were still asleep.

Without knowing what time it was, it was hard to determine if she should wake them up now or wait. She went down the stairs. Finally, she found a clock hanging on the kitchen wall. It was almost 5:30.

She heard a sound from behind her and jumped when she saw Bill wheeling himself into the kitchen. She put her hand over her heart and chuckled. "I didn't realize you were up."

"I'm used to getting up early. Henry usually comes around this time to get the kids up and ready to go to town." He came further into the room and went to one of the shelves on the wall that had been built for the height of the wheelchair. "I can't tell you how excited I am to get a house in town. It takes so long to get to town in a wagon. When I could walk, I'd go on my horse. The ride was much quicker."

She bet it was.

"Do you mind making a pot of coffee? I ground the beans and put them in here." He selected a small bag and held it out to her.

She accepted it and loosened the bag where the smell of freshly ground beans greeted her. "This smells expensive."

"I get a discount since I'm the owner of the store I buy it from." He winked at her. "The pot is on the shelf of the cookstove. All you have to do is pump the water into the sink."

"Alright." She went to the cookstove and lit the coals to warm it up. "What do you want to do for breakfast?"

"Henry brought in some eggs last night. You mind frying them up?"

"No. Eggs are easy."

"They are, but not everyone likes them. There's a loaf of bread and some butter in that box on the counter. Vernon will only eat the bread, so don't make any eggs for him."

"How much food should I make for the children? Do they eat as much as adults?" Even as she asked the question, she felt silly. She'd shared two meals with Amber and Vernon but hadn't taken the time to watch how much they ate.

Fortunately, he didn't make a snide comment. Instead, he said, "No, they don't eat much. Amber only needs one egg. I think between the two of them, three slices of bread will do. They can each have one-and-a-half buttered slices." He chuckled. "Don't set the butter in front of Vernon. He'll pick up the whole thing and try to eat it."

She grimaced.

"I know," he agreed. "I don't understand how he likes it all by itself, but he treats it like candy."

She filled the pot with water then she set it on the stove. Placing the bag on the table, she turned to him. "I have time to wake the children up before the coffee's ready. Then I can make breakfast. Is there anything special I need to do to help them get ready for the day?"

"Just wake them up. Amber will take care of Vernon. It might not seem like it, but she can do a lot for a seven-year-old. The poor thing had to grow up faster than other girls her age."

She caught the regret in his voice and understood why he felt that way. No child should have to lose a mother, and the same child shouldn't be expected to fill in a mother's role because her father was confined to a wheelchair. But the selfish part of Deanne was glad the girl was mature for her age. It helped to have someone around here who could help her with a four-year-old boy.

"I won't be long," she told him before she left the kitchen.

"THAT WILL BE $3.56," Deanne told a customer later that day.

The mother with four children sorted through her coins while her oldest, a boy who looked to be ten, helped Deanne put the items his mother had purchased into two large boxes.

The door opened, and Deanne saw two old ladies enter the store. "I'll be with you in a moment," she called out to them.

Once the mother was done putting the coins on the counter, Deanne quickly counted them then put them in the leather pouch. She slipped it into the pocket of her apron.

"I'll carry one of the boxes out for you, Mrs. Wibaux," Deanne said.

The mother began to reply, but one of her children called out to her, so her attention went to the girl. Deanne picked up a box and went around the counter. The mother followed behind with the other box. The boy, thankfully, opened the front door. All mothers seemed to be busy. Ever since her marriage to Bill, she found herself paying attention to women who had children with them, especially children who were the same age as Amber and Vernon.

Once she put the box in the woman's wagon, she returned to the store and hurried over to the two ladies who were looking through a catalogue.

"May I help you?" Deanne asked.

"Good morning, dear," one of the ladies said. "I'm Winnie Jordan, and this is my sister, Piper Miller."

Since the ladies looked expectantly at her, Deanne obliged them by saying, "I'm Deanne Harvey."

"Harvey? Are you Bill Harvey's new wife?" Piper asked.

Deanne nodded. "We just married yesterday. Is there something I can help you with?"

Winnie's eyes lit up with excitement. "So it's true then. Bill did take another wife. We heard the rumors about a wedding at the preacher's house yesterday, but we weren't sure they were true."

"We had to come and see for ourselves," Piper added.

"Where are you from?" Winnie asked.

Deanne glanced from one woman to the other, and it occurred to her that they hadn't really come here to purchase something. They were here to satisfy their curiosity. Since it would be rude not to answer the question, Deanne said, "I'm from Omaha."

"All that way?" Piper asked, her eyes wide.

"Omaha isn't that far," Winnie replied. "There are places farther than that. Like New York and Chicago."

"Yes, those places are farther. That's a good point," Piper said. "But even so, it does take time to get from Omaha to here. It's not like she was already in town. She wasn't even on a nearby farm."

"If she had been, we would have already known who she was." Winnie's gaze went back to Deanne. "Did you come here because of the ad Bill posted looking for a wife?"

"Oh yes, we knew about that ad." Piper giggled. "You're a lucky girl. He's a good man."

"Handsome, too," Winnie added.

Deanne shifted uncomfortably from one foot to another. "Yes, well, he wanted someone who could add and subtract numbers quickly."

"Yes, I know he was looking for permanent help at this store," Winnie said. "Archie couldn't be expected to do this for years on end. He's our age, and we can only handle so much before we get tired."

"You get tired more easily when you're our age," Piper told Deanne. "A young thing like you wouldn't know anything about that. Speaking of which, how old are you?"

Deanne glanced at the door, hoping someone who was an actual customer would come by, but since that didn't happen, she said, "I'm thirty-one."

"Oh, thirty-one," Piper began. "Is this your first marriage?"

"No," Deanne replied.

"So you're a widow like poor Bill," Winnie said. "How many children did you have from your first marriage?"

Deanne hated these questions. Why did everyone assume that just because she was a woman, it meant she could have children?

Before she could figure out a way to answer them that wouldn't lead to them asking why she hadn't had children, Bill came out from the back room.

"How are you doing, Winnie and Piper?" he greeted.

The two women left the catalogue and went over to him.

"It's good to see you, Bill," Winnie said. "Piper and I thought we'd come by to welcome your bride to Lincoln."

"Yes, we were excited to hear you married again," Piper added.

Deanne should have been relieved Bill had taken their attention off of her, but she couldn't help but be annoyed. Why couldn't everyone mind their own business like Mrs. Wibaux did? Not once did that woman ask Deanne anything personal. She'd kept everything strictly to what she wanted to buy.

"You two knew I was looking for another wife," Bill told them, his tone indicating that he was amused rather than annoyed like Deanne was.

"Yes, but we didn't know you found her," Winnie replied. She glanced at Deanne. "She's very pretty."

"Yes, she is," Bill said.

Despite the compliment, Deanne decided to put the catalogue away. She didn't feel up to idle chitchat. All the two women were going to do was spread everything they learned around town. Then who knew if others would be coming to the store to look her over. It was like living in that apartment with Mrs. King all over again.

"How did the children take the marriage?" Winnie asked him.

"They took it very well," Bill replied. "I've been preparing Amber for a new mother, and Vernon doesn't remember Jennifer."

Winnie put her hand over her heart. "Yes, the poor dear. But maybe that's for the best. He'll adjust to this change faster than Amber will."

"Amber will be fine," Bill said. "This will be good for her. She's taken on too much for a little girl."

"She has," Piper agreed. "She's pretty much been your legs at home."

Deanne glanced at Bill, wondering if he was taken aback by the comment, but he didn't seem to mind. If it was Deanne, it would have bothered her if someone pointed out the fact that she couldn't do as much as others because she was bound to a wheelchair.

"I'm fortunate that God gave me a daughter who does so much for her little brother," he said.

"That's the way to look at it, Bill," Winnie replied with a nod. "Amber is a sweet girl. I'm sure she's going to have men lining up to court her."

Bill chuckled. "I'm not ready for that yet. I'd like to keep her little for a while longer."

"Enjoy every minute of it while she and Vernon are still children," Piper said. "They grow up so fast. I don't know how time slips away from those of us who are older. Children seem to be so impatient to grow up, but all we have to do is blink and they're already adults."

"Yes, it's hard to believe we're both already grandmothers," Winnie replied.

"Great-grandmother," Piper said. "I just found out my oldest granddaughter is expecting."

Winnie gasped. "She is? Why didn't you tell me sooner?"

"I was going to say something after we welcomed Deanne to this town," Piper replied. "I didn't want to take away from the newest member of the community."

As if they all remembered Deanne was in the room, everyone looked at her.

Deanne's face warmed. What did they expect her to say?

Bill broke the awkward silence. "Deanne and I appreciate you coming by to welcome her here."

Deciding that was a good response, Deanne said, "Yes, thank you."

"We shouldn't keep you two from your work," Piper replied. "I remember Archie saying he had his hands full when he was working here. It was nice meeting you, Deanne. And it was good to see you, Bill."

Deanne smiled at them but was relieved when they went on to ask Bill a few more questions. It allowed her to pretend to be occupied as she straightened things on the shelves.

Once the women left, Bill called out to her. Deanne turned her attention to him, surprised he hadn't returned to the back room.

"Did they make you uncomfortable?" Bill asked.

"No."

"Something's wrong. I'd like to know what it is."

"Nothing's wrong. I'm just new here. People are curious." No matter where she went, people always seemed to be curious.

"They didn't mean any harm in coming by."

"I realize that." They never meant any harm. They were all just nosy. She wished they could all mind their own business. She didn't go up to strangers and ask them a bunch of questions. She let them live their lives as they wished. It was a shame no one let her live her life as she wished. It'd be nice to have the freedom to do something without someone judging her.

"I'd like to start this marriage off on the right foot," Bill said, his voice soft. "If you don't want to talk about what's bothering you, I'll respect that. I just want you to know I'm willing to listen if you ever want to talk."

He turned to go back to the room, and she breathed a sigh of relief. She really didn't feel like getting into an argument, especially not on the day right after they married.

The front door opened, and this time someone came into the store who actually wanted to buy something. Relieved, she turned her attention back to her job.

Chapter Six

"DO I HAVE TO EAT THIS?" Amber asked that evening as she stared at the beans on her plate. "I hate beans. They're smushy."

"I think you mean 'mushy,'" Marsha said.

Amber looked at her and crossed her arms. "They're gross. I hate them."

"They're good for you," Bill spoke up. "Besides, you like the taste."

"But they feel wrong when I eat them," Amber said.

"There aren't a lot of beans on your plate," Bill replied. "Eat them, and you can have dessert."

Amber looked over at the plate of cookies as if trying to decide whether or not eating the beans was worth it.

Deanne couldn't blame her. While she understood that Bill wanted his daughter to eat what was on her plate, she also sympathized with a girl who didn't like the texture of beans. She had no idea what to do in a situation like this. She glanced at Henry who didn't even look up from his plate. He just continued eating as if this happened all the time. For all she knew, it did. But this was the first time she'd seen this.

"It's up to you," Bill continued. "You can choose not to eat them. No one will make you. But you also have to understand that if you choose not to eat them, you won't get any cookies tonight."

Amber glanced at the cookies again, and after a moment, she picked up her fork and ate the beans.

Deanne's gaze went to Bill. He'd handled that very well. She liked that he gave the girl a choice. He hadn't banged the table and demanded she eat the beans like her father would have done.

After supper, Deanne helped Marsha wash the dishes while Henry got the wagon ready and Bill watched the children.

Marsha chuckled as she washed one of the cups. "Amber always says she hates beans, but every time, she'll eat them."

"She does?" Deanne asked in surprise. If this was the case, then why did she make it a habit of complaining about them?

"I don't make them a lot. I try not to make things the children don't like. It's just that I had so much to do today that it was easier to let the beans sit in the pot while I did other things."

"You can get things done while watching children?"

"Once you get used to them, you figure out a routine that allows you time to do other things. Little Roy Hanson ripped his pants, so I wanted to mend them. He lives with his grandparents, and his grandma's hands hurt too much to hold a needle anymore."

Deanne was curious about what happened to Roy's parents, but she opted not to pry. If she didn't want people snooping into her business, she wasn't about to do it to others. She turned her attention back to the pot she was washing and scrubbed the bottom clean.

"Life must seem pretty quiet out here compared to Omaha," Marsha said.

Deanne shrugged. "I don't know. I stayed busy at the store today. It seems like plenty of people go out and do things."

"Yes, but I wager it's not as much as what people do in Omaha. Isn't Omaha bigger than this town?"

"It is." The difference in the train station sizes had startled her at first when she arrived in Lincoln, but then she recalled that her hometown in Kentucky was even smaller. "I keep busier here. I never worked when I lived in Omaha."

"Most women don't work. They stay home and take care of their husbands and the little ones. You'd be doing that, too, if Bill was able to run the store by himself."

Deanne suspected if he could run the store by himself, he wouldn't have remarried. He already had children, and his aunt watched them while he was at work. There wouldn't be a reason to take a wife.

"I like you," Marsha said.

Surprised that the woman should come out and say that, Deanne glanced at her. "You do?"

"You've got a quiet gentleness about you. I can see why Bill picked you. He had quite a few offers."

"I bet he did." Even with a wheelchair, he was a handsome and sweet man. What woman wouldn't be drawn to that?

"I think you'll be good for him. He doesn't complain. It's not in his nature. Even when Jennifer died, he didn't question why. He just said that there's a purpose for everything and that it's not up to us to question why God allows bad things to happen. We just have to trust that He knows what's best."

Well, that was a big difference between her and Bill. Deanne often questioned why God allowed bad things to happen. Though, to be fair, she was the one who'd made the decision to answer a mail-order bride ad from a stranger in Omaha. God hadn't been responsible for that mistake or the problems that had come with it. She could only hope this was one decision she'd managed to get right. She finished scrubbing the pot then rinsed it out.

"I complained about Jennifer's death," Marsha softly said. "I'm not strong in the faith like Bill is. I questioned it every day for the longest time. I even got angry. It's not fair when people go before their time, and it's even more upsetting when they leave people behind who need them." Her gaze went to Deanne. "I wish I could say I'm strong, but I'm not."

"You shouldn't feel bad," Deanne said when she noted how disappointed Marsha was with herself. "I question things, too. I think it's normal for some of us to be weaker than others."

Marsha gave her a grateful smile and wiped her eyes with the edge of her apron. "Look at me. An old woman who is getting all worked up when there's nothing to get worked up over. Things turned out just fine. You're here now. Bill will have a companion to share the rest of his life with, and the children will have a mother. God did have a plan."

Deanne wasn't sure what that plan was but nodded for Marsha's sake. Afterwards, she set the clean pot aside and grabbed another dish to clean.

A WEEK LATER, BILL was finishing up balancing the ledger when Deanne stepped into the back room of the store. He glanced up from the desk. "What is it?"

"Mr. Brown would like to see you," she said.

"Send him in." Bill marked his place as she left the back room. He closed the ledger and set it aside. He grabbed the leather pouch with the money in it just as the middle-aged man came into the room. "Hi, Morgan. I'm glad you came by. This was starting to get too full to close."

Morgan smiled and took it before he sat across from him. "I heard you married again, but I didn't realize your new wife was so pretty."

"You can't have her. I married her first."

Morgan chuckled and settled back into the chair. "I'm glad you finally got someone who can help you all the time. I know this job took a toll on you when Archie was here."

"Archie did a good job."

"Yes, but he had trouble keeping up with the pace that's needed to manage a store. There are three customers out there right now, and your wife didn't even flinch when I came in. She handles herself very well."

Bill's left eyebrow arched. "Since you're so interested in her, I'm surprised you didn't stop by sooner like the others did."

"I was on a business trip."

"That explains it. How did it go?"

"Boring, but most bankers are boring to talk to. I'm glad to be back."

"What about Kansas City? That wasn't exciting?" Bill asked.

"It's no fun going around a city when you're all by yourself. I stayed in the hotel room when I wasn't at the meetings. It might have been better if any of the books I'd brought with me were interesting."

Bill shook his head. "I told you to take some of the dime novels. They're actually pretty interesting."

"I don't know. It's hard to think of them as real books. The binding is different, and they're cheap."

"You can't let factors like that dissuade you from trying at least one. They sell very well in this store. As soon as a new shipment comes in, they're almost all gone within a week."

"I don't believe it."

Bill nodded toward the leather pouch. "Fifteen percent of the money I made was from dime novels."

The man opened the pouch, and his eyes grew wide. "You're putting me on."

"Nope. It's true. People can't get enough of them. Even the stories for children sell well, and you'd be surprised to know that it's not only children who read them."

"I believe you. The money in this pouch doesn't lie. But I have something more interesting to talk about than dime novels. I found someone who is looking for a farm to buy. He's a young man with a wife and child. They recently came out West for land to farm on, and I told them they might as well buy a farm that is ready to go than start with just a piece of dirt. Do you mind if I take them out to your place?"

"No, please do." This was good news. "When you come back, will you let me know if they're interested?"

Morgan rose from his chair. "I'll let you know. They're still waiting at the bank."

"Are there any houses available in town?"

"There are a couple. If that man wants the farm, do you want to take a look at the houses today?"

Bill nodded. "The sooner I can move into town, the better."

"I don't blame you for being anxious. It can't be easy going back and forth almost every day, especially when you're in a wheelchair."

"It will be nice to wheel myself out of the house and down here." Bill hadn't realized how much he'd taken the ability to jump up and down on a horse any time he wanted for granted. "It'll be nice for my aunt and uncle, too. They still have to watch my children while Deanne and I are here in the store. At least this way, she and I can pick them up and go home."

He was sure they'd still have dinner with his relatives. He couldn't see putting Deanne through the hassle of making dinner after she spent all day working here. Her role was different from what Jennifer's had been. While she was alive, he'd been able to hold down this place all by himself.

"I'll come back later today and let you know what happens." Morgan lifted the pouch. "I'll also return this so you can fill it up again."

"Thanks, Morgan."

Morgan offered a nod and left the room.

Bill heard Morgan tell Deanne goodbye on his way out. He hoped the couple wanted the farm. It'd been so long since anyone expressed an interest in it that he'd almost given up hope. He was beginning to worry he'd end up having to desert the place. He couldn't give up the store. It was the only way he made money. Sure, people on farms were able to grow food, collect eggs and milk, or sell animals to make ends meet. Jennifer had been good at making a little extra to add to their finances by tending to most of the farm work. He, however, had grown up in town. He never did manage things on the farm as efficiently as she had. But he could operate a store. This was something he knew like the back of his hand, and it was something that made him comfortable.

He took his ledger back out and finished working through the receipts. Then he organized the receipts into their respective folders and filed them away.

By the time he was done cleaning his desk, Morgan returned with a wide grin on his face. Bill blinked in surprise and glanced at the pocket watch resting on his desk. He hadn't been aware so much time had passed. And Deanne hadn't come back once to ask him for help. She had required his assistance a few times over the past week, but it seemed like she had everything under control now.

"I have good news," Morgan said. "They want the farm."

Bill's ears perked up. "They do?"

"Yep. Conner is working with them on the loan as we speak." He gave Bill the pouch. "Is it too late to look at houses? We can always do it tomorrow if now is a bad time."

"Let me check with Deanne." Bill backed the wheelchair up and then wheeled along the ramp that went to the front part of the store.

Deanne was in the middle of collecting money from Archie's daughter, Maybell, who had five-month-old Calvin strapped to her chest with a cloth-made sling.

Bill's eyebrows rose in surprise. "Where's your husband and pa?"

Maybell glanced over at him and grinned. "Hi, Bill. Jack just acquired a couple of cattle, so he and Pa are branding them. It's just me and Calvin today."

Calvin was blabbing and looking all over the store in interest.

Bill smiled. "Well, the boy doesn't seem to mind being dragged all the way into town."

"He loves being in the buggy," Maybell replied.

"My son and his wife had a little one last year," Morgan said. "Enjoy the time when they're like this. They grow up so fast. Before you know it, he'll be running all over the place."

"I'm enjoying this time very much," Maybell assured him.

"It's not so bad when they get older," Bill said. "I like it when they can tell me what they want. It's better than guessing."

"You always were a practical one, Bill," Morgan replied with a chuckle.

Bill smiled in amusement then turned his attention to Deanne as she finished giving Maybell the change. "Morgan says someone is interested in the farm. I was thinking of looking at some houses in town. What do you think of closing the store early and joining me?"

"You want my opinion?" Deanne asked in surprise.

"You're going to live there, too," he replied.

"You should go," Maybell told her. "It's fun to go into people's houses and see where all the rooms are."

As if he wished to offer his agreement, Calvin squealed.

"I'll take the box to your buggy, Maybell," Morgan offered with a chuckle.

Maybell thanked him as he picked it up.

Bill glanced at Deanne and saw that she was putting the money into the pouch. "Will you put that in the back?" Bill asked her. "I'll turn the sign to let people know we're closed and head on out."

Deanne offered a nod, and soon they were on their way to look for their new home.

Chapter Seven

DEANNE FOLLOWED BILL and Morgan into one of the houses in town.

"This is all on one floor," Morgan said. "It's smaller than the others, but I think it might suit someone who's in a wheelchair. It only has two bedrooms. If you had more little ones, I know someone who can help you add another room to this house."

Deanne clasped her hands together but forced herself to remain quiet. Why did everyone assume all women could have children?

"The parlor looks nice," Bill said as he scanned the empty room with a fireplace and dusty floors. "The window is large. I like that. It lets in plenty of sunlight." He glanced at Deanne. "What do you think?"

Deanne felt herself relax at the gentle tone in his voice. "I like the large window."

"If you like lots of light, you'll love the kitchen," Morgan said. "Two windows are in there, and it overlooks the backyard. The yard has a fence, Bill. Your children will be able to play there without running off."

Since Bill looked at her expectantly, Deanne left the room first and followed Morgan to the kitchen, which, as he had promised, had plenty of light. The yard was a good size. She thought Amber and Vernon might like playing there. They might even one day like climbing the large tree. She remembered how fun it'd been to climb trees when she was a child.

"Is this a new cookstove?" Bill asked.

She turned her attention from the window and watched as Bill opened the oven door.

"It might as well be. It's only a year old," Morgan said.

"It looks like it was hardly used," Bill replied. "Was the previous owner someone who didn't like to cook?"

"Mrs. Quincy did cook, but she was also a meticulous housekeeper," Morgan said. "The only reason there's dust is because it's hard to convince people to come to Lincoln. Most people want to go to Omaha. That's where all the big stores and restaurants are."

Bill nodded.

Morgan was right. One of the reasons Deanne had chosen to marry Terry was that he'd been in a big enough city to offer things she'd never had in her small Kentucky town. She'd figured even if the marriage wasn't that great, she would still enjoy being in a big city. In the end, it hadn't made any difference.

"Mr. Quincy loved working with his hands," Morgan continued. "He put this dining cabinet in here."

Deanne turned her attention to the large oak cabinet in the corner of the room. Morgan opened the glass doors to show them the shelves and then pulled open the drawers.

"Mr. Quincy also put in the countertops and sink." Morgan went to the handle over the sink, and after a few pumps, water came out. "He knew how to do quite a few things. One might consider him a jack-of-all-trades." His gaze went to Deanne. "I think you'll like the improvements he made around here. Mr. and Mrs. Quincy moved to Iowa. They have one daughter. She's married to a farmer out there. A few months ago, they decided to move out there so they wouldn't miss being with their grandchildren."

Deanne offered a smile, though she had to resist the urge to groan. Again, more children and grandchildren. Was there no one but her who wasn't able to have them?

"I didn't realize they moved for that reason," Bill said.

"I only know because they gave me this house to sell on their behalf," Morgan replied. "They'd be glad to have this off their hands.

But," he lifted his hand and grinned, "I don't want to put any pressure on you. We have a couple more houses to go to." He glanced between them. "Would you like to see the other rooms, or have you lost interest?"

Bill looked at Deanne. "Do you like what you're seeing so far?"

"Yes," Deanne said. "I'd like to see more of it."

Bill nodded then turned his gaze back to Morgan. "You said there are two bedrooms?"

"There are," Morgan said. "They're this way."

Deanne followed him and saw that the windows in the other two rooms had more space in them than it seemed from looking at the house from the outside.

"The windows are easy to open," Morgan said as he went over to one and lifted it.

The wind swept into the space and cooled the hot room.

"It's easy to adjust how much you want it open, too," Morgan added then demonstrated this fact. He glanced at Deanne. "Do you want to try it?"

She shook her head. "That's not necessary. I can see how easy it is."

He shut the window. "The fireplace in the parlor has been cleaned out and is ready to use." He paused then added, "I think that's all unless you got any questions."

Deanne had no questions, so she glanced at Bill.

"Can I get a ramp put in at the front and back doors?" Bill asked.

Morgan nodded. "I can get those set up if you take the place, but I advise you to check out the other two houses first."

"Part of whether or not I put in a vote for this place all depends on if I can get a ramp," Bill told him.

"I can arrange for a ramp to be put in at any house you pick. That's an easy thing to do," Morgan replied. "The nice thing about most of the houses in town is that all the rooms are on one floor. You got a couple that have an upstairs and a downstairs, but for the most part, they're all suitable for someone in your condition."

Well, that was good news. While it might make picking the house Bill wanted more difficult, it would be nice for him to have more than one place to choose from. Deanne had already decided she would pick whatever house Bill wanted. It didn't matter to her what kind of home she lived in. What she wanted most was to be content, and being content was more about the people she was around than the kind of roof that was over her head.

They left the house and went with Morgan to the other two houses, and in the end, she realized that Bill had liked the first house they went to the most. It had larger windows, the nicest backyard, and the cookstove that was practically new. When Bill asked for her opinion, she picked that one. Bill seemed happy, and he made arrangements to meet Morgan at the bank tomorrow to sign the paperwork for the home. She was glad for him. Soon, they would be living here in town, and he would be spared the hassle of always going back and forth to town in a slow wagon.

Now he could wheel himself to the store and to his house. That would give him a greater sense of freedom and independence. Those were two valuable things, and being here with Bill, and seeing the world through the perspective of someone who was bound to a wheelchair, she was beginning to understand how wonderful those things were.

A FEW DAYS LATER, AMBER turned to Bill as Henry and a couple of other men brought in a few more pieces of furniture into their new home.

"I don't want to live here," Amber told Bill. "I want to go back home at the farm."

Bill and Amber were in the corner of the parlor so they could be out of the way of the men. Vernon was with Deanne and Marsha in the kitchen. From the way things smelled, they were brewing coffee and cooking something. He had thought Amber might want to run in and join them, but she'd chosen to stay with him in the parlor.

"I know you miss your mother, honey, but I can't stay all the way out there on the farm anymore," Bill said. "You remember what I told you about my legs. I can't walk, and it gets hard to go back and forth to town all the time."

"But Mama was there," she said.

"Yes, she was. Just because we're going to a new home, it doesn't mean we'll leave her. She's still right here." He tapped her heart. "And here." He tapped his heart. "No matter what happens, no one can take that away from us. We don't need a house for that."

She let out a sigh that told him she didn't like the answer but wasn't going to argue his point. He didn't know what else he could say, so he grew silent. He hadn't thought this move was going to be hard on Amber, but she did remember her mother. That house must have been a comfort to her in ways Bill hadn't realized.

He caught sight of a crate filled with the things he and Jennifer had once kept in their bedroom. An idea came to him. "Would you like to put your mother's picture in your bedroom? The photograph was taken when she was sixteen. There's a lot of her in you. I bet when you're sixteen, you'll look like she did."

Her eyes lit up. "I want to see it."

"Henry!"

Henry stopped on his way to one of the bedrooms. "Yes, Bill?"

"Is that picture of Amber's mother from when she was sixteen in there?" Bill asked as he pointed to the crate.

"I think so." Henry sorted through the things in it. "Ah, here it is." He pulled it out. "You want this?"

Bill nodded and held his hand out to take the picture that was in a wood frame. Bill turned to Amber and showed it to her. Then he studied his daughter's face. "I can't believe how much you two look alike."

Amber smiled. "I like that I look like her."

"I do, too. It's a good reminder that she was a part of our lives. In addition to looking at her picture, you can also look in a mirror."

She hugged the picture to her chest. "Can I get a mirror put in my room?"

He nodded. "We can arrange that."

Her smile widened, and he felt better for her. It was nice that Amber could smile when she thought of Jennifer. The good memories of Jennifer's life should outweigh the pain of losing her. And who knew? Maybe having Deanne would help the girl. Every girl should have a mother to raise her and teach her how to be a young woman. He hoped that, in time, Amber would grow to think of Deanne as her mother. He didn't expect Deanne to replace Jennifer, but it would be nice if Deanne could pick up where Jennifer left off.

Marsha came out from the kitchen. "We just put cookies in the oven. Is there anyone who would like one when they're done?"

"That's not fair, Marsha," Henry said as he rubbed his stomach. "You know I've been trying to avoid eating sweets."

"You can say no," Marsha replied.

"How can I say no to cookies?" he asked.

"Easy. You say, 'no'. No one is going to force you to eat one. Besides, I was talking to everyone." She gestured to Bill, Amber, Morgan, and Jack.

Henry groaned. "You know baked sweets are a weakness of mine. Why can't you stick with something I won't be tempted by? Like cabbage. Why not offer us cabbage?"

Bill grimaced. "No one thinks of cabbage as a treat."

"Exactly. That's my point," Henry said.

"I'll eat your cookie for you," Amber told him.

Amber looked so proud of herself for thinking to help him by eating his cookie that the others chuckled.

Bill patted her back. "That's alright, honey. I'm sure Henry will manage to eat one. Why don't you put your ma's picture away and go into the kitchen to help set the table?"

With an enthusiastic nod, Amber hurried to her new bedroom.

"I can't believe that girl tried to steal my cookie," Henry said, eyes wide. "You ought to keep an eye on her, Bill. Now that you got a wife, you might find that your sweets will go missing around here."

Bill laughed then went to Amber and Vernon's new bedroom so he could help Amber find a place to hang the picture.

Chapter Eight

DEANNE DIDN'T KNOW why she had assumed Bill would sleep in the parlor after they moved. She should have known that the only reason she had slept alone in bed before was because he couldn't go upstairs in a wheelchair. But such a thing had not occurred to her, and it was with a mixture of shyness and uncertainty that she watched him come into the bedroom that evening. She had already put on her nightgown and had braided her hair so it wouldn't tangle through the night.

"Amber and Vernon are finally asleep," he said as he took the hardbound book off of his lap and set it on the dresser. "I think it's going to take them a few days before they can go to sleep at bedtime."

She moved aside so she wouldn't get in his way. She had no idea where he intended to go, and the room wasn't that big, even though there was plenty of room for him to get around the bed.

"It's hard for anyone to sleep well in a new place," she said as he took off his tie and vest. She cleared her throat.

He glanced at her. "Are you alright with me sleeping in here?"

"This is your bed. You can sleep in it."

He set the pocket watch on the dresser then turned the wheelchair so he was facing her. "I didn't mean to make you nervous. I assumed it would be fine to be in here."

"It is fine," she insisted, aware that there was a slight tremble in her voice even as she spoke the assurance. "I've been married before. I've shared a bed with another person."

"There won't be anything that happens in the bed. All I plan to do is sleep. I thought I explained that."

At once, she felt much better. She didn't know why the thought of being intimate made her so nervous, except that it would expose the truth about her inability to have children.

"You said you were fine if there wasn't anything of a physical nature between us," Bill softly said.

"I am fine with it," she hurried to reply. "I meant that. I just thought that since you slept in the parlor at the other home, you'd do so here, too. It shocked me that you came in here."

She thought she saw his hands relax on the arms of the wheelchair. Was he nervous, too?

"The bed is more comfortable than the couch," he said after a moment.

"That's true. I'd rather sleep on the bed than the couch. No one can blame you for wanting to be in here." She hesitated to offer help since she wasn't sure if it would make things more awkward than they already were, but finally, she asked, "Would you like me to help with anything? I can get your side of the bed ready for you and put the wheelchair next to the bed after you're settled in."

"Actually, I wouldn't mind some assistance getting into the bed. It's higher than the couch. It'll probably be a challenge to get in."

"I can help." She'd much rather do something than just stand by and watch. "What would you like me to do?"

He hesitated then said, "After I get my nightshirt, I'd like you to help me get into the bed. I'll use the arms of the chair as much as possible so I don't overwhelm you with my weight."

"I'll pull back the blankets so the bed is ready while you get your nightshirt."

He nodded, and at once, she felt the tension in the room ease. She couldn't blame him for feeling awkward. She felt it, too. He probably wasn't used to asking for help. Sure, he had accepted it from his aunt and uncle, but other than that, he seemed to do everything by himself. It couldn't be easy for him to allow someone new to do what came so naturally to everyone else. As for her, she had no idea how to help someone who was in a wheelchair. It wasn't something she'd ever had to do before.

She didn't know if the children would wake up, but she shut the door so that if they happened to come to this room, they wouldn't have to see their father struggling to get into the bed. She knew if it was her, she wouldn't want anyone to see her needing help with this kind of task.

She went to the bed and pulled the blankets back and then fluffed the pillow. By the time she was ready, he had his nightshirt resting on his lap. He wheeled over to the bed and backed up so that he was parallel with it. She didn't think the task was going to be all that difficult once she realized the bed was only slightly higher than the chair.

"Do you want to put one of your arms around my shoulders?" she asked.

He set the nightshirt on the pillow and nodded. "That seems to be the best way to do it. It's what Henry did for me right after the accident." He locked the wheels then straightened up. "I'm ready."

She bent down to assist him. As he had promised, he put most of his weight on the arm of the wheelchair as she helped him onto the bed.

"I didn't tell you what happened to my legs, did I?" he asked, surprising her.

She shook her head. "No, but you don't have to."

"I don't mind telling you. As you know, I lived on the farm. After Jennifer died, I tried to continue running it. I didn't do much, but I did plant a couple of small crops. One day while I was on the tractor, I leaned over to grab my hat when it blew off." He shook his head. "It was the stupidest thing I could have done, and I knew better, but I didn't think things through. Anyway, I fell out, and the back tire ran over the bottom part of my legs."

She winced. "That sounds painful."

"The funny thing is that I didn't feel the pain right away. It wasn't until I couldn't stand up that I realized something was wrong. It was then that I started to feel the pain. Fortunately, Marsha was out on the farm watching the children. If it wasn't for her, I don't know how long I would have been out there in the field."

"I'm sorry it happened."

"Thank you, but it's fine. I accepted the way things turned out. I'm just glad the children are alright and that people keep buying things at the store. I'm also glad you've been married before because this whole thing would be even more awkward if you were a virgin."

"Really? How so?"

"I was thinking it might be nice to have help getting the pants off. That part always takes the longest whenever I go to bed. It's also a struggle to put them on, too."

She offered him an understanding smile. Of course, a woman who wasn't used to seeing a man without clothes would shy away from the task. "I'll be happy to help with that."

And she did help him. She tried to avoid looking at his legs as she helped him out of the drawers and pants, but her curiosity got the best of her and she took a peek. His legs had been cut off just below the knees. She could only imagine how hard it would be to live like this. So as not to embarrass him, she hurried to put away the clothes he'd been wearing that day.

"Would you like me to keep the window open?" she asked since she couldn't think of anything else to say.

"I like the fresh air, but it can get chilly in the early morning hours," he said after he had the nightshirt on.

She glanced at the window. "What if I leave it partly open? That should prevent the room from getting too cold."

He nodded. "Let's do that."

She went to the window and lowered it down. By the time she got into the bed, he was already settled into a comfortable position. It was strange to be in bed with someone again after having gotten used to sleeping by herself. Fortunately, the bed was big enough to accommodate them both so she didn't have to be pressed right up against him. That eased the situation somewhat. Knowing they wouldn't be doing anything but sleeping further relieved her nerves.

"It's much more comfortable in the bed than the couch," he said. "It's been so long since I slept in this bed that I'd forgotten how nice it is."

"It is a comfortable bed," she replied. "I don't think I've ever slept in a better one."

"I almost didn't get it since it was more expensive than most, but Jennifer assured me it would be worth it since I wouldn't have to replace it for a long time."

She supposed she shouldn't feel uneasy about sleeping in a bed that Bill used to share with another woman, but she did. It almost felt like she should be the one sleeping on the couch. Unlike her marriage to Terry, Bill and Jennifer had loved each other. This bed probably brought him good memories of her.

"Are you alright?" Bill asked.

How did he have a way of picking up on her mood when she was uncomfortable? It was a bit spooky. "I'm fine," she replied.

"So seeing my legs the way they are didn't bother you?"

Was that what he thought? Her eyebrows furrowed. Did he worry she was repulsed by the fact that he didn't have all of his legs? She turned her gaze to him. "I already knew you had part of them amputated when I first saw you in the wheelchair." Her face growing warm, she added, "I was curious about what amputated legs looked like without pants covering them up. I've never seen anyone without a limb before."

"It took me a while to get used to it."

"I bet it did." Anyone would struggle with not having all of their legs. "I don't care that you need a wheelchair, and I don't mind helping you whenever you need it. To tell you the truth, I like that you let me help you, whether it's at the store selling things or here at home in this room. It gives me a purpose. I don't like sitting around and doing nothing all day. I prefer to keep busy."

"Are you sure you like keeping busy at the store? It seems like you barely have a moment to sit down for a good portion of the day."

She chuckled. "Time goes faster when there are customers in the store."

"Yes, but you also have to put items away when a new shipment comes in. You also have to clean up the place."

"That doesn't bother me. When I'm done, it's nice to see the store looking nice and tidy. It gives me a sense of accomplishment."

He reached over and took her hand in his. "I can't imagine any other woman being as good as you are in that store. I'm glad you made the trip from Omaha."

Her skin warmed more from the pleasure of his words than the gentleness of his touch. She couldn't recall a time when anyone had given her such a high compliment. She searched her memories, but nothing came rising to the surface. Surely, she must have received kind words in the past. It'd just been so long ago that it was difficult to remember them.

"Good night," Bill whispered.

He released her hand and turned onto his side to go to sleep.

She turned onto her side and closed her eyes. The warm feeling stayed with her all night.

Chapter Nine

THE NEXT MORNING RIGHT after Deanne helped Bill put on his pants and get into his wheelchair, she went to wake the children. After she got Vernon dressed, Amber came up to her with a hairbrush.

"Can you make my hair look like my ma's?" Amber asked her.

Deanne's gaze went to the black and white picture of a girl who wasn't even twenty yet. "That was your mother?" she asked Amber.

Amber nodded. "She was pretty, wasn't she?"

"Yes, she was." Though the girl in the picture wouldn't be marrying for another couple of years, Deanne could see why Bill had been attracted to her. Forcing aside the thought, she brought out the wooden chair in the corner of the room and encouraged Amber to sit in it. "I haven't fixed anyone's hair in a long time. I'll do my best, but I can't promise I can get it to look exactly like your mother's hair."

Since Amber seemed content with the promise, Deanne collected the pins and a couple of ribbons from the little box on the dresser. "Would you like a certain color?"

Amber studied the ribbons. "The orange one is pretty."

"We'll do the orange one then." Deanne didn't think she would need a second ribbon but kept the assortment out, just in case.

Vernon picked up his blanket and ran out of the room with it.

"Someday, he won't need the blanket anymore," Amber said.

"Did you once have a blanket you liked to take around the house with you?" Deanne asked as she brushed the girl's hair.

"I did when I was a baby, but I'm a big girl now."

Deanne didn't think a seven-year-old was that old, but what did she know? Maybe in child years, seven was old. After a long moment of silence, she asked, "Do you remember very much about your mother?"

"I have three memories of her."

When the girl didn't continue, Deanne asked, "Do you want to tell me about them, or would you rather keep them to yourself?" If the girl didn't want to tell her what the memories were, Deanne didn't know what else they could talk about, and the room was going to be filled with an awkward silence.

Thankfully, Deanne's sudden burst of panic was for nothing because Amber said, "I'll tell you. One was when Ma took me to the chicken coop to gather eggs. I got to put them in the basket for her." Judging by the way Amber grinned, Deanne got the impression that this was a big deal for a child. "I like that memory best. I got to carry the basket into the house, and I didn't drop it. Ma was happy."

Deanne smiled as she put the brush down and retrieved some pins. "That's a good memory. I can see why you like it."

"I think about that memory a lot. Then I have a memory about kittens being born. Cats are good for getting mice, so you want them on a farm."

"Your pa said something about that on the day I married him."

"I helped Pa take food out to them after Ma died. You want to feed them enough to keep them around, but you can't feed them too much or they won't eat the mice."

Deanne nodded and started pinning the sides of the girl's hair up.

"Not all kittens make it," Amber said. "One time when I was helping Ma when kittens were being born, one died as I was holding it. Ma said it was too little and that made it weaker than the others. That is a sad memory."

"I'm sorry you lost the kitten."

"I am, too, but losing Ma hurt more."

Deanne didn't know what words she might have to offer that would help with a hurt so deep, so she did the only thing she could think of: she put her hand on the girl's shoulder and offered her a sympathetic smile.

To her surprise, the girl returned her smile, assuring her that she had given her a good response. Feeling better, Deanne returned to pinning her hair up.

"The last memory is when Ma was holding Vernon. He was so tiny he couldn't even sit or walk," Amber said. "I was afraid she'd stop loving me because he was smaller and cuter than me."

"There's no way she could ever stop loving you," Deanne said. Even if she didn't have children of her own, she couldn't imagine a single mother who could stop loving her child.

"She didn't stop loving me. I know that because she took me out to the chicken coop soon after that."

Oh, so that further explained why Amber's favorite memory involved bringing in the eggs. "I'm glad your mother let you carry those eggs."

"I am, too. It was fun."

Deanne finished with the last pin and picked up the orange ribbon to weave into her hair, careful to do it as close to the picture as she could. When she was done, she encouraged the girl to look at the mirror. "Is there anything you'd like me to change?"

Amber inspected her reflection with surprising scrutiny, and Deanne was beginning to think she was going to have to redo the girl's hair when Amber said, "It's perfect! How did you get it to look just like Ma's picture?"

Deanne shrugged. "I did my best."

There was a loud knocking on the front door, and Deanne hurried to go to it. To her shock, the door was partly open, and the older woman was holding the doorknob so that it wouldn't fling all the way open as she knocked on it. The woman stopped when she noticed Deanne.

"Are you the mother of the children who live here?" the woman asked.

"Oh, um, yes," Deanne replied, doing her best not to flinch at the woman's sharp tone. "I'm Mrs. Harvey."

"Mrs. Harvey? You're the one who married the owner of the general store?"

Deanne forced a nod. Whatever was coming next wasn't going to be pleasant. The woman was still speaking sharply to her.

"I suppose I won't speak to the sheriff since I heard you have no children of your own," the woman said. "I can't expect you to know what to do with them so soon after marrying Mr. Harvey." She straightened up. "You ought to be aware that the boy was peeing out in the yard where everyone could see him."

"He did what?" Forgetting the woman's tone, she hurried to the door and went out on the ramp.

Vernon had the blanket wrapped around his shoulders and was running around the yard.

"He's not doing it now, but I assure you, he was," the woman said from behind her. "We have outhouses in the back yards for a reason, and there are things like chamber pots he can use."

Deanne turned her gaze back to her, not knowing what she could say. No one had ever come up to her to complain about a child before.

"Can I help you?" Bill called out.

Deanne looked over at Bill as he wheeled himself over to them.

The woman left Deanne's side and headed straight for Bill. "You need to mind your son, Mr. Harvey. He was out there acting as if the front yard was an outhouse or a chamber pot. There are little girls outside playing this time of day. They don't need to see something like that. It's inappropriate."

"I haven't had a chance to talk to Vernon about that yet," Bill said. "We used to live out in the country, and he's made it a habit of doing that since no one was around to see him."

He did? Why hadn't Deanne noticed? It never occurred to her that children wouldn't use an outhouse or a chamber pot. She just assumed they knew to do that.

"Being in the country is no excuse," the woman argued, her hands on her hips. "He should not do that here."

"I understand," Bill said. "We only moved in yesterday, and then we were all tired and went to bed. It's my fault. I'll talk to him today. It won't happen again."

"Make sure that it doesn't," the woman replied, still sounding upset.

Deanne blinked. What else did the woman expect Bill to do? It wasn't like he could turn back time and stop Vernon from going out there. Nor could Bill do anything beyond talking to the boy.

"Next time, I'll get the sheriff," the woman said. "This is a respectable community. We need to keep it that way. If you want to stay here, you'll remember that."

Deanne noticed the way Bill's hands clenched the wheels on his wheelchair, but he kept his tone calm as he said, "It won't happen again. Vernon's a good boy."

The woman let out a "humph" then left the house.

Recalling that Vernon was still out there, Deanne hurried to pick Vernon up before the woman could snap at him. Deanne might not have children of her own, but she understood enough to know that they didn't think things through like adults did. Vernon hadn't meant to be indecent.

The woman hurried across the street, and Deanne watched to see which house she went to. It was the one to the left of the house directly across from hers. Good. Now that Deanne knew where the woman lived, she'd be sure to avoid that house.

She went back inside and set Vernon down. She was sure it wasn't her place to tell Vernon what to do, so she decided to tell Bill she'd make breakfast and then hurried to the kitchen.

A COUPLE OF HOURS LATER, Deanne was counting out the change to give to a middle-aged male customer when Bill emerged from the back room. She glanced his way.

"When you have a moment, can I speak with you?" Bill asked her.

She nodded then turned her attention back to the customer.

"You seem to have gotten the hang of running this store pretty fast," the man said.

She smiled as she finished counting out the change. "I enjoy it. It's easy to figure things out when you're enjoying yourself."

"You're much better than Archie. I like him and all, but he had a tendency to just want to stand around and talk. Not only did it take longer to get out of here, but half the time, he gave me incorrect change. This," he added as he pocketed the coins she gave him, "is exactly what I'm owed. Thank you, Mrs. Harvey."

"Thank you," she replied, pleased by the compliment he'd just given her.

After the way the morning had gone with that grouchy woman across the street, it was nice to hear something positive. Bill hadn't said anything about the incident, but she could tell he'd been upset. Unlike her first husband, he hadn't started yelling or grabbing some whisky to calm down. He hadn't even blamed Deanne for letting Vernon go out to the front yard. Bill had just explained to Vernon that he couldn't answer nature's call on the front lawn. The only indication she got that he was upset was the fact that he'd been quieter than usual during breakfast. By the time they came to the store, he was back to his normal self.

It was nice to be with someone who wasn't given to fits of rage when he was upset. She hadn't known a man could keep calm despite an unpleasant situation. It was no wonder Jennifer had fallen in love with him.

Since there was no other customer at the moment, Deanne went to the back room to see what Bill wanted.

Bill was waiting for her at the desk with a piece of paper in his hands.

"You wanted to talk to me?" Deanne asked.

He nodded. "Every three months, Ross Henderson likes to come here to get this very long list of things." He held the paper out to her.

She went over to him to take it and scanned the items. Her eyes grew wide as she went through everything on it.

"I know. It's a lot," Bill said. "Archie used to get my uncle's help. Ross will be by at two. He always comes in at two. He only comes in every three months because he's got a lot going on at his farm. He has seventeen children."

"Seventeen children?"

He chuckled. "I know. Even I can't wrap my mind around that one. It seems that his wife is always having another one. I wouldn't be surprised if he says she's expecting the eighteenth one when he's here."

"I didn't know it was possible to have so many."

"Apparently, it is. I don't even think they have to be intimate for her to conceive. He can probably just look at her from across the table and it happens."

She smiled in amusement at his joke. "Or maybe the kids just grow in the fields."

He chuckled. "Maybe they do. Anyway, that's why the list is so long. Ross tries not to come to town any more than he has to."

"I wouldn't, either, if I was him." Between Amber and Vernon, she felt that things were busy enough at home. She couldn't imagine fifteen other children to take care of.

"You should get my uncle to help with that list," he said. "I don't expect you to do it all by yourself. Even when I could walk, I had help with large orders like that. My uncle will be at the livery stable. Don't worry about taking him away from his job. There are others who can fill in for him while he's gone."

"Should I put a sign at the door to let people know I'll return soon?"

"No, I can handle anyone who comes in for the short time you'll be gone."

"I'll be back as soon as I can," she promised then hurried out of the store.

On her way to the livery stable, she was surprised at the number of people who called out a greeting to her. Yes, they had greeted her when she'd been with Bill, but she had assumed they'd only said hello because of him. Very few people had said anything to her in Omaha when she left the apartment by herself. Though, looking back, she hadn't left the apartment much, and most of the time when she had, she'd been with Terry.

She hadn't thought about it until now, but Terry had been insistent that she be with him as much as possible when in public. He had said a pretty woman shouldn't be out on her own, even if she was married. While she supposed he had paid her a compliment, the way he'd treated her hadn't given her a reason to feel all warm and fuzzy from his words. She'd only felt the same silent frustration she'd experienced in Kentucky where everything was managed for her. If she hadn't kept the mail-order bride ad a secret from her family, they would never have let her leave.

She had hoped that being married would allow her more freedom, but with Terry, it hadn't. Perhaps he had worried about her having an affair because that's what he had done. As far as she could recall, he hadn't slept with another woman during the first three years of their marriage. It wasn't until a woman came to her apartment and asked if she was Terry's sister that she began to suspect Terry wasn't really at work when he claimed he had to put in some overtime.

She forced away the memories. She was glad she wasn't in Kentucky. She was glad Terry was dead. It might be a mean thing for a woman to think. She was sure if anyone knew, they would think she was bad. One was supposed to think well of their family and the dead.

But what good would it do to lie to herself? She didn't have to voice her thoughts aloud, but she had a right to think them, didn't she? Especially in light of the fact that Bill was giving her freedom to run an errand without telling her how to do it.

Yes, she was glad Terry was gone. She didn't want to have anything to do with him. She was much happier now. She had no idea that when she answered the ad for the interview, she was going to marry someone much better. She hadn't even been aware people like Bill even existed.

So what if there was a crotchety woman across the street who made it a habit to tell other people what to do? At least she was in another house. Deanne didn't have to live with her. She didn't even have to say hi to her if she happened to see her. She could go into her house and pretend the woman didn't even exist. If that woman was the worst she had to deal with, she was a very blessed person.

Within minutes, she found the livery stable, and after she found Bill's uncle, she returned to the store, her steps lighter than they'd been since she could remember.

Chapter Ten

THE NEXT MORNING, DEANNE made sure to take Vernon out to the backyard so he could relieve his bladder in the outhouse. He tried to go by the tree, but she insisted he go in the little building instead.

"Pa doesn't do it," Vernon protested.

"Your pa can't do it," she said, keeping her voice low in case anyone over the fence could hear them. The fence was tall enough where she couldn't see into the yards of the neighbors, but she had learned from experience that just because you couldn't see someone, it didn't mean they weren't listening. "Your pa is in a wheelchair because he can't walk. You have to be able to walk to get into that small privy."

Vernon stared at her for a moment then asked, "Can he pee?"

She was caught off guard by the innocent question, but she supposed if she was a child who didn't understand how the human body worked, she'd wonder about it, too. After all, if someone couldn't walk, what else weren't they able to do?

"Yes, he can do that," she softly said. "He just uses a chamber pot. We have a couple of them. Would you like to use one instead of going to the privy?"

He furrowed his eyebrows so seriously that she found it cute. It made him look much older than his four years. He glanced at the privy then said, "I don't like the pot. It stinks."

Well, he was right about that. Having lived in an apartment, she had learned to tolerate the smell when she had to clean the chamber pots. Looking back, she was glad for it since it had prepared her for taking care of Bill's chamber pot. At the farm and here, she used the privy only because it saved her time in cleaning them. Bill had been cleaning his own, but she'd insisted on doing it for him since she could do it in far less time than he could.

And that's why he had married her, wasn't it? To help him out? Her duties as a wife didn't stop when they left the general store. Given how much better things were with him than they'd been with Terry, she didn't mind. If she could make Bill's life easier by helping him with anything, she would do it simply out of gratitude.

Vernon went to the privy and opened the door. He stood there for a long moment. She watched him in interest. Just what was he looking for?

He looked back at her. "I'll go in here."

He said it in such a matter-of-fact way that she couldn't help but chuckle.

She waited until he was done and led him back into the house. "We'll have breakfast soon."

"What will we eat?"

"I was thinking of making eggs and seasoned potatoes this morning."

His nose wrinkled.

"Do you want something else?" she asked.

"Pie," he replied.

"I can't give you pie this early in the day."

"Why not?"

"Pie isn't something people eat in the mornings," she said. "They eat things like eggs, seasoned potatoes, pancakes, oatmeal, bacon, ham." Out of ideas, she added, "Do you want pancakes? We can put some syrup on them to sweeten them up. That's a little bit like a pie."

"I never thought of pancakes that way before, but I suppose they are like having dessert in the morning," Bill called out.

She went to the kitchen and peered into it. "I didn't know you were listening to us."

He grinned as he put ground coffee beans into the coffee pot. "I hope you don't mind."

"No, I don't mind." He wasn't someone she wanted to keep things from. "Do you want pancakes?"

"I'll eat anything. I'm easy to please. Just make whatever you want," he told her.

She turned her gaze to Vernon.

"I want morning pie," he said. "Pancakes with syrup."

"Well, they aren't really a pie, Vernon," she said.

"You just said they were," Vernon replied, his eyes wide with shock.

"I said they were a little bit like pie when you put syrup on them," she corrected.

"Pies are sweet," he said. "I want sweet."

Bill laughed. "It's alright with me if we call them morning pies."

She felt herself relax. It probably didn't matter how Vernon chose to think of them. The important thing was he was willing to eat them. "I'll be happy to make them," she finally told Vernon.

He let out a cheer and ran into the parlor where he jumped up on the couch and peered out the window. She hoped he didn't leave the house, but if he did, at least she knew he wasn't going to upset that grouchy woman across the street by using the front yard as a privy.

Bill put the coffee pot on the table. "I'll go out there and watch him while you make pancakes. If he goes outside, I'll be there in case someone complains about something he's doing."

"You mean you'll be there in case that woman complains."

"It's possible she'll find something else she doesn't want him doing."

"I hope she doesn't come back here. I hate dealing with difficult people."

"You handle yourself well when people bother you."

"I know how to keep my mouth shut, but it's not easy."

"It's never easy."

She hesitated to say what was on her mind, but since he had a gentle way about him, she admitted, "I noticed that you remained pleasant even though you were upset yesterday morning."

"In my experience of working at the store, it's people who make it a point to complain that are miserable deep inside. I was angry, but I also decided that just because she's miserable, it doesn't mean I have to be. To be honest, I feel sorry for her. It would be terrible to spend each and every day finding reasons to complain about something."

Deanne hadn't thought of things that way before, but he was probably right. People who had a tendency to complain were probably miserable. Terry did a lot of complaining, and he never seemed to be happy, no matter what people did for him.

"Life is too short to waste it on things you don't like," Bill said. "You might as well focus on things that bring you joy."

She watched him as he wheeled himself into the parlor. He was right. If more people spent time thinking on things that were pleasant, they would be better off for it. And that included her.

"Will you help me with my hair again?" came a girl's voice from behind her.

Deanne turned and saw Amber holding a brush and the same orange and white ribbons they had used yesterday. She glanced at the clock and saw they were doing good on time. "Sure."

She called out to Bill and Vernon that she would start the pancakes after she finished with Amber's hair then followed the girl to her bedroom.

Amber hopped into the chair. "I looked pretty yesterday."

"Of course, you did."

"I look like my ma."

Deanne glanced at the photograph. "Yes, and she was a pretty woman. I'm not surprised you're pretty, too." Deanne set the ribbons aside then started to brush her hair. "I'll try to be careful not to hurt you as I go through the tangles. Your hair is so thick. Maybe we should put your hair in a braid at night so that it's not tangled in the morning."

"Are braids pretty?"

Amused by the question, Deanne said, "I'm not sure if they're pretty, but they are practical. They keep the hair smooth and soft during the night. When you wake up and brush your hair, it won't hurt your poor scalp." Deanne winced as she worked her way through a tangle. "I'm sorry."

"I know you're not hurting me on purpose," Amber said.

"I'd still feel better if we tried the braid. Just for tonight. If you don't like it, we won't have to do it again."

"Alright." After a few seconds of silence passed, Amber asked, "Do you wear a braid at night?"

"I do. Then I brush my hair in the morning and pull it back into a bun at the nape of my neck. A bun is another way to prevent the hair from getting tangled. It also helps you keep cool when it's hot and you need to do a lot of work."

Amber turned to face her in interest. "How long is your hair?"

Deanne thought for a moment and then put her hand on the midpoint of her back.

Amber's eyes grew wide. "That long?"

Deanne nodded.

"Why don't you wear it down?" the girl asked.

"Like I said, it gets hot. Maybe when winter comes, I'll wear it down. It has to be cool enough so I don't end up sweating all the time. When a man sweats, no one thinks anything of it. But women aren't supposed to sweat. It's not ladylike."

"I didn't know that."

"It's an unspoken thing. No one would publicly say it."

"What other things don't people publicly say?"

Deanne picked up the two ribbons as she thought of some more examples. After a moment, she said, "Well, it's impolite for a woman to burp, but if a man does it, it's just one of those things men do."

"Vernon burps a lot," Amber replied. "It's gross."

Deanne smiled at the disgusted look on the girl's face.

"If I had a sister instead of a brother, it wouldn't be like that," Amber added.

"That's not true. Girls and women do the same thing. We just learn how to hide it so no one notices. Though, I don't think it's possible for a woman to burp as loud as some men do."

"I've never heard Pa burp."

Deanne had noticed that, too. Bill was nothing like Terry. "Your pa is a gentleman."

A pitter-patter of footsteps echoed through the house, followed by Bill telling Vernon to get back into the parlor. However, Vernon kept running and came into the room.

"I'm starving," Vernon said, clutching his stomach. "When can I eat morning pie?"

"I'll start them in five minutes," Deanne promised the boy.

"Get back in here," Bill called out.

"It won't be long," Deanne assured Vernon.

Vernon ran back to the parlor, and his feet made the same pitter-patter sound off the hard floor.

"We can't have pie in the morning," Amber said as Deanne put the ribbons in the girl's hair.

"We're having pancakes," Deanne replied. "I told your brother that they are sweet like a pie when you add syrup to them. He's decided to call them morning pie."

Amber rolled her eyes. "That must be another silly thing men do that women don't."

Though Deanne was sure that doing something silly like calling pancakes a morning pie wasn't restricted to men, she found the girl's comment so funny that she ended up agreeing with her.

When Deanne was finished, Amber ran to check her reflection in the mirror, and Deanne hurried to go to the kitchen so Vernon wouldn't have to wait much longer for breakfast.

Chapter Eleven

A COUPLE WEEKS LATER, Deanne was totaling a customer's order when Bill came out from the back room. She glanced over at him as he passed her. She turned her attention back to totaling the cost of the items on the list the customer had given her.

Usually, people came in for a small order, but this man had come in with a long one. The man looked familiar, but she had trouble remembering who he was. So many customers came in and out of the store during the course of the day that it still overwhelmed her at times, though she had to admit it was getting easier.

The man turned to face Bill and tipped his hat.

Bill offered a wave.

When Bill didn't say anything, Deanne remembered that the man in front of her was Pete, and Pete couldn't hear. She wondered if Bill had heard her speaking to Pete. Maybe that was why he had come out here. Maybe he wanted to stop her from making a fool of herself in case another customer came into the store.

Face warm, she totaled up the last two items, and then she worked on adding everything together.

Pete stood in front of her, and thankfully, he seemed to have all the patience in the world since his expression remained polite.

When she was done adding everything up, she showed the amount to Pete.

Pete offered a nod then dug his hand into his pocket. He pulled out a few bills and quite a few coins. She was ready to count the money for him when he started doing it himself.

"If you put one of the crates in my lap, I'll collect some of the things he wants," Bill told her.

With a nod, she retrieved a crate from under the counter and set it on Bill's lap. She tried not to make eye contact with him, but when his hand brushed hers, she instinctively did so. He smiled at her and patted her hand. She was so startled that she couldn't respond.

"Can you show me the list so I know what to put in here?" he asked.

Breaking out of her shock, she nodded and showed him the list Pete had given her.

Bill scanned it then handed it back to her. "I'll get the things within my reach. You get the rest."

She cleared her throat. "Alright."

He went over to a shelf by the window and put a container of coffee grounds into the crate.

Recalling Pete, she returned to the counter. He had finished putting the money on the table. She quickly sorted through it and gave him his change.

He tucked it into his pocket, gave her a smile, and then picked up the crate she had planned to use. He gestured to the items on the high shelves that he wanted then pointed at himself.

Not sure what he wanted, she glanced at Bill. "Do you have any idea what he wants?"

Bill turned his gaze to Pete who looked at him and pointed to the items he wanted on a higher shelf and then pointed to himself.

"I think he's asking if he can get the things high up by himself," Bill said. "Nod that it's fine."

Deanne did, and Pete's smile widened before he started to put some of the things on his list into his crate.

"It's not every day a customer comes in who wants to help out so much," Bill said. "It's actually kind of nice."

"Yes, it is." She took out another crate from under the counter then admitted, "I forgot he was deaf. You must have thought I was foolish when you came out here and realized there wasn't anyone else in the store."

"No, I didn't think that. Pete does a good job of getting along with people as if he can hear. Once he's been in here a few more times, you'll remember him. I know it takes time to get used to people's faces. When I started working here, I got people's names wrong all the time." He chuckled. "I'll never forget the time I called this woman Frankie. It turned out that Frankie was the nickname she had given her husband. Those two didn't let me forget it for a whole year." After a moment, he added, "Do you want to know what her name was?"

"What?"

"Quinn."

She felt a smile tug at her lips.

"It's alright to laugh," he said. "It is funny."

She gave herself permission to laugh. "I can understand why you mixed their names up. I would have assumed Quinn was the husband's name, too."

"You're doing a wonderful job, Deanne. I hate to say it, but you're almost doing too good of a job. I came out here because I was bored. There's nothing else I have to do at the moment. You don't interrupt me in order to get me to help you with something out here." He winked at her. "I'm not complaining."

Her skin warmed in pleasure from the compliment, and she turned her attention to the list so she could help collect the things Pete had purchased.

"I WONDER IF THE STORE might be better laid out if we moved this table over there," Bill said the next day when there was a lull in activity.

Deanne stopped lining up the dime novels on the shelf and glanced his way. "I thought you were going to organize the buttons and threads in the sewing section," she said in amusement when she noted that he was on the other side of the store. She placed her hand on her hip and feigned indignation. "I think you're looking for a reason to get out of working."

He smiled at her joke. "I can get back to organizing later. This table is bothering me."

She walked over to the table which had bags of flour, baking soda, and cornstarch on it. "This table has been in this spot since I first came here. Why is it only bothering you now?"

"I didn't notice where it was until I was in the sewing section. It makes more sense if the cloths for sewing are over here. I was thinking that this table would be better placed by the fruits and vegetables on that side of the store."

She followed the direction he pointed to and saw the small table holding tobacco, pipes, and cigars that was next to the fruits and vegetables. "Where would you put the tobacco, pipes, and cigars? They don't fit next to the sewing supplies."

"That's a good question." He left the spot where he was at and wheeled himself across the store.

The store had been arranged to allow him enough room to get from the back room to the front door, and that was pretty much it because some of the tables were angled in a way that he couldn't pass through them. She wondered if he had stopped to consider this before he started winding his way through the small aisles.

When he ended up getting trapped between the display of jars containing jams and jellies and the barrels of potatoes and preserved meats, she hurried to push one of the barrels aside.

"Sometimes it's frustrating that I can't move around easily like I used to," he muttered as he backed up.

"There's not much room in here."

"No, there's not, but I can't afford a bigger building." When he was back in the wider aisle, he added, "It sure would be nice if everything wasn't so cramped."

Her heart went out to him. She knew what it felt like to be restricted from doing something she wanted to do. She used to envy some of the women who could come and go from their apartments whenever they wanted. It wasn't until she came here that she felt she could go anywhere in town without getting her husband's permission. Also, it was nice that she was able to go wherever she wanted without having to maneuver a wheelchair around.

"If it will help, I can push some things aside so you can get through the store easier," she offered.

He let out a sigh. "Some of the barrels and sacks are heavy."

"All I have to do is scoot them along the floor. They aren't so heavy when I do that. Then you can wheel yourself through here and see where everything is located."

"That's a lot of unnecessary work. It would just be easier to have you go through the store and call out where everything is."

"I can do that."

She waited for him to tell her where he wanted her to go, but to her surprise, he asked, "Doesn't it bother you that I can't walk?"

"Why should it bother me?"

"Because I'm not like other men. I can't do a lot of things by myself. I need your help to move things around this store. I need your help to get in and out of bed." He rolled his eyes. "And I don't want to even think of the chamber pot."

"Bill, I don't mind helping you with those things. That's what I'm here for. I'm your wife."

"I know you're my wife, but other wives don't have to do all of this for their husbands. The most they're asked to do is take care of the children, keep the house clean, and have meals ready at reasonable times."

"Some husbands don't ask their wives to do anything. Some husbands demand they do things. They dictate every hour of the wife's day. They tell her where she can go and who she can talk to. They tell her what to wear or how to style her hair. And if they don't have a good day, they act as if she's the one who ruined it for them. I'd rather have someone like you than what I used to deal with."

His eyes widened in surprise. "I didn't realize you had a bad marriage with your first husband."

She shrugged. "No one does. They all assume Terry and I were happy because married couples are supposed to be happy. Sometimes I envy you. Your first marriage was a good one."

"My second marriage is a good one, too," he softly told her.

She blinked in surprise. It was?

She didn't know what to say. His expression was so tender that it made her heart leap with hope. She knew he had loved his first wife. She didn't think there might be a chance he'd love her, too.

She was spared from having to give a response when the door opened and two women entered the store.

Bill hesitated but turned his attention to them. "Good afternoon, Jody and Eunice." Bill moved his wheelchair so he could face them. "How can we help you today?"

As the women answered, Deanne pushed aside the strange flutter in her stomach. Now wasn't the time to dwell on how this second marriage was going. She didn't know how to properly think through their conversation at the moment anyway. She needed time to sort things out. The women had offered her a reprieve.

She took a deep breath then went to help Bill take care of the customers.

BY THE END OF THE DAY, Deanne had reorganized the items in the store so that they would be easier for the customers to find. It never ceased to amaze Bill how much Deanne could do. He'd had several men help him with this store since getting it, and he couldn't think of a single one who was more efficient than her. She had been born for this job.

She really was a lovely woman. Quiet and gentle. She didn't ask for anything. She was eager to do whatever she could to help, and that went for the store and at home.

Also, it warmed his heart to see how nice she was to his children. He knew he'd been taking a risk when marrying because not all women were kind to their stepchildren. He was sure a good number of them were. Women seemed to have a natural mothering instinct about them. In the small town of Lincoln, there weren't a lot of widowers with children who remarried, but he recalled how cold Jacob Wilson's second wife had been to his son. She'd taken care of the boy well enough, but everything she'd done had been out of obligation, rather than sincerity.

Deanne might seem uncertain at times about her role as a mother, but she wanted to be a good one. He didn't know if she realized it or not, but his children were already developing an attachment to her. Amber didn't let just anyone touch her hair. The girl was particular about who she let do anything to her. So the fact that Amber was asking Deanne to decorate her hair was significant. As for Vernon, he sure enjoyed those morning pies at breakfast. Thinking about how Vernon kept calling the pancakes that made Bill chuckle. The way to that boy's heart was through his stomach. Yes, Bill knew Deanne and his children would get along just fine.

Up until today, Deanne hadn't said anything about her first marriage. Bill hadn't known why he'd assumed it had been like the one he'd had with Jennifer. He knew some men could be strict with their wives, but he'd never heard of one who went so far as to dictate what his wife wore, how she styled her hair, where she could go, or who she could see. Though Deanne's voice didn't convey her resentment at being treated that way, he'd noticed the way her face hardened when she'd talked about her first husband.

At that moment, he realized he didn't have to feel like he was such a burden to her by having her do things for him he was unable to do by himself. He hadn't consciously worried about any of it until he'd gotten stuck in that aisle. When he realized he couldn't get out without her help, all of the embarrassment and awkwardness he'd suppressed had come rushing to the surface. It was to his relief and surprise that he realized she really didn't mind helping him. She didn't consider him to be less of a man because he was in a wheelchair.

In that moment, he realized that he was falling in love with her. He hadn't expected such a thing to happen. When he posted the ad for a wife, he was looking at things from a practical standpoint. He figured he would be offering the woman a place to stay and his protection. Meanwhile, she would help him raise his children and operate the store. He had seen it as a partnership, one in which he had hoped would result in friendship. But somewhere along the way, it had become deeper than that.

And now that he'd realized he felt the stirrings of love, he couldn't go back to just thinking of her as someone who was here to help him with the store and his children. Things would change now. They wouldn't change because he was going to will them to; they would change because they had to. Once someone became aware that their feelings had changed in a given situation, it was impossible to stop the process. The feelings would continue to change and adjust.

He looked up from the desk in the back room where he'd been trying—unsuccessfully—to fill out the list of supplies he needed to order. From the front of the store, he could hear Deanne talking to a customer about a recipe the woman was thinking of trying. His lips curled up into a smile. That was a conversation he'd never heard when Archie was helping someone.

He lowered his gaze back to the paper in front of him, but no matter what, he couldn't focus on it. The conversation he'd had with Deanne earlier that day kept going through his mind, and, as silly as it seemed for a man in his mid-thirties, he had the strange compulsion to spend time with her. He'd thought he was over such schoolboy longings after he fully matured, but apparently, even grown men could entertain youthful fantasies.

He glanced at the pocket watch which was resting on the desk. It would be time to close the store soon. He could work on this tomorrow. He set the paper in the top drawer then left the room.

Chapter Twelve

"I WAS THINKING," MARSHA said that evening during dinner, "Amber's old enough to go to school."

Deanne glanced at the girl who was sitting beside her. The girl was busy eating the chicken on her plate. The comment didn't make her look up. Deanne glanced at Marsha and saw that she had directed the comment to Bill, which was good since Deanne didn't know when children were old enough to go to school.

Bill swallowed what he was eating and studied the girl. "What are the ages of the children who are at the schoolhouse?"

"Some start at six, but I heard an eight-year-old just started this year. Amber's a smart girl, and I think she gets bored staying here with me all day."

"I'm not bored," Amber said, looking as if she was afraid that being bored would get her in trouble.

Marsha and Henry laughed while Bill smiled in amusement. Deanne supposed it was funny that the girl was worried, but Deanne wondered if school was something necessary for children so they didn't get bored. It didn't seem to her that Amber got bored. Amber spent a lot of time watching over her brother or playing with her dolls when she wasn't helping Deanne or Marsha in the kitchen.

Deanne reasoned that she didn't notice the boredom since she was at the store with Bill most of the time. Now that she thought about it, she had been bored in Omaha. An apartment was small. There was only so much a woman could do before she ran out of work to keep her occupied. Perhaps it was like that for children.

"No one is upset with you, Amber," Marsha assured the girl. "It's just that your time would be better spent learning how to read and do math than being here all day."

Amber's eyebrows furrowed. It took Deanne a moment to realize the girl was trying to decide whether she believed Marsha or not. Deanne felt the corner of her lip curl up. It was cute. She didn't know why it'd never occurred to her that children weren't all the different from adults. Yes, they were younger and they had much to learn, but they experienced the same emotions adults did.

"You like books," Marsha told Amber. "Imagine if you could read them by yourself instead of waiting for me to read them to you."

Amber's face relaxed, and Deanne could tell that Marsha's strategy worked. Amber had decided Marsha had a good point. That was interesting. So children, at least those Amber's age, could reason through the benefits of learning how to do something. An adult didn't necessarily have to tell them to do something. An adult could point out why something was in their best interest.

"I'd like to read books," Amber said. "When do I start school?"

Marsha's gaze went to Bill, and Deanne found herself looking to Bill as well.

"When do children start school?" Bill asked.

"They start in September," Marsha replied.

"But that's a long time from now," Amber said. "I want to start reading now."

"Oh, well, you won't learn to read right away," Marsha replied. "Even when you start school, it'll take time to learn."

Amber sighed in disappointment.

Deanne couldn't help but feel sorry for her. The girl had gotten excited about learning to read. It wasn't her fault she didn't know learning to do that would take time. If Deanne knew the right words to say, she'd say them, but the only thing she felt qualified to do was offer a simple gesture, so she rubbed the girl's back.

"I can start teaching you a little bit now," Marsha told the girl. "That way, you'll know something when you start school."

Bill's gaze went to his daughter. "The time will go fast. You'll be starting school sooner than you think. September isn't that far away. On some days, I can't believe you're already seven."

"That's the way it goes," Henry spoke up. "The older you get, the faster time goes. I remember when I was a kid. I thought time went so slow. I didn't think I'd ever grow up. And look at me now. I'm getting gray hair."

"Oh, you've got plenty of time left," Marsha assured him as she gave him a playful swat on his arm. "I'm as old as you, and I'm plenty young."

He gave her a wink. "You haven't aged a day since we married."

Deanne watched the exchange in interest. She had come to understand that they had a good marriage. It was probably similar to the kind of marriage Bill had enjoyed with his first wife. For all she knew, they had inspired Bill to be the kind of husband he was. She thought back to her parents, and while they never argued in front of her, she didn't recall any sweet gestures like the ones she was seeing between Henry and Marsha.

With her parents, the arrangement had seemed to be more like a necessary arrangement. She hadn't thought about it until now, but there had been no warmth in her house while she was growing up. Her marriage to Terry hadn't been much different. She was tempted to glance at Bill, but she couldn't bring herself to do so. After what Bill had said to her earlier that day, she had a reason to think this marriage might be more like the kind Henry and Marsha shared. But she was almost afraid to get her hopes up too much in case she ended up disappointed. She learned long ago it was best to avoid expecting too much. There was a lot of pain to be had in disappointment.

The conversation turned to what Henry had done at work that day. Relieved since it gave Deanne something else to think about, she concentrated on what Henry was saying as she continued her meal.

THAT EVENING AS DEANNE was tucking the children into bed, Bill sat in the wheelchair by the dresser. He had removed everything but his pants. That was as much as he could do on his own. As on other nights, he had to wait until Deanne was in the room so she could help him into the bed.

Apparently, Vernon had already drifted off to sleep since Amber was the only one he heard talking to Deanne, and from what little he gathered since he couldn't make out everything Amber was saying, the girl was curious about what school was like. So that was why Amber was unusually chatty this evening.

He supposed it was natural for her to want to find out everything about school tonight. What child wouldn't want to know exactly what to expect? The more the girl knew, the less apprehensive she would be.

It wasn't just children who had a difficult time sleeping when confronted with something new. If he was honest with himself, he felt as restless as his daughter did. Except, it was for different reasons.

He had put aside the part of him given to romantic desires and passions on the day of his accident. Yes, Jennifer had died, and he hadn't touched another woman, but the option to remarry and share the more intimate side of things had been there. But when the doctor told him he would never walk again, he figured things like romance and passion were over forever.

Today, however, Deanne gave him hope that, despite his injuries, he might be able to resurrect that part of his life. For the first time in a very long time, he didn't only feel like half a man. He felt whole again. Being with her had completed him in a way he hadn't expected it to when he married her.

He supposed that shouldn't scare him. He'd been married before. It wasn't like he didn't know how this worked. But he couldn't remember the last time he'd had an erection, and until today, he hadn't had any desire to have one. He wasn't even sure he could have one now.

He heard footsteps coming down the hall. He waited to make sure they were heading in the direction of his bedroom before he wheeled himself over to the bed. While he might not be able to get into, or out of, the bed by himself, he wanted to do everything he could to make things easier on Deanne. Maybe since her first husband had been an overbearing and demanding person, she didn't mind doing the less-than-ideal tasks for him, but he saw no reason to add to the tasks he was asking her to do.

She opened the door to their room and gave him an apologetic smile. "Amber didn't want to go to sleep. I had no idea when your aunt mentioned school to her, she'd get so excited about it. She wanted to know what schooling was like for me." She shut the door behind her and pulled down the blanket and sheet on his side of the bed. "I'll help you in."

"I didn't mind waiting," he assured her as he put one arm around her shoulders and set his free hand on the mattress. "I could tell she was wide awake when you took her and Vernon to their bedroom."

"While I appreciate you being a patient man, the hour is getting late. The children get to sleep in longer than you do."

"You get up early, too."

"I don't require much sleep to feel alert through the day."

She pushed him toward the bed, and he shifted so that he was able to relieve her of the bulk of his weight before he got too heavy for her. Once he was sitting on the bed, she helped him out of his pants. Then she brought the sheet and blanket up to his waist. As he did on other nights, he put on the nightshirt.

Usually, he got settled onto his back as soon as he was in the bed, but tonight, he decided to watch her.

"How much do you want the window open?" she asked as she went over to it.

He shrugged. "Maybe a couple of inches. The breeze is coming in pretty good."

She nodded and lowered it.

"What was school like for you?" he asked.

"Alright. I can't remember anything special about it. I spent a lot of time reading."

"Really? I would have thought you worked on arithmetic all the time since you're good at it."

She gave him an amused smile. "I loved arithmetic, but the teacher never thought I'd do anything with it. He did, however, think I was going to spend a lot of time reading bedtime stories to my future children. I'm sure he'd be shocked to find out I'm helping you run the general store."

"Yes, well, I'm sure he didn't think you'd marry someone confined to a wheelchair. You've done a lot to help me with the store. You did a good job organizing the store today. It looks much better now."

She beamed at him, and he was struck by how much her first husband had taken her for granted. He didn't really want to know the details of her first marriage. The glimpse she'd given him had been enough. He would rather focus on her and the future they had.

After Jennifer's death, he'd spent plenty of time in the past. The days after his accident had given him even more time to relive those days he'd had with her. The day he realized that dwelling on everything he'd lost was causing him to neglect his children, he made the decision to go on with his life. Jennifer was gone. There was nothing he could do to bring her back. But he was still alive, and he, despite being bound to a wheelchair, had a responsibility to be the father his children deserved.

He went through the motions at first. He read the books Jennifer had saved from her childhood so a part of her would be passed on to them. He watched them play and helped them with the simpler tasks one could do from a wheelchair. He listened to Amber ramble on about everything she and Vernon had done during the day while he was at work.

It took a while for the emotions to catch up to his actions, but one day as Amber was running after Vernon so he'd put on his shoes, he burst out laughing. She'd had the same look of disbelief that Jennifer had when she was overwhelmed. It was so funny to see that expression on a child's face. That was the first time he felt happy since Jennifer's death. And, from there, more moments came until he woke up one morning with a feeling of gratitude that he was still alive, and from there, he decided he was going to look at things to be thankful for instead of thinking of the things he didn't have.

He was blessed to have two children who were in good health and happy. He was blessed to have Uncle Henry and Aunt Marsha who did so much to help him. He was blessed to have people like Archie who had given him assistance when he'd needed it at the store. He was blessed to have customers who made the longer parts of the day pass by faster when they came in to talk. And he was blessed to have Deanne. He couldn't have asked for a better wife after Jennifer died.

He brought his attention back to Deanne and watched as she finished braiding her hair. She kept it up during the day. The style was attractive. It wasn't a tight bun like he'd seen some women wear. She allowed some strands to fall to her shoulders. He found it curious that even when she braided her hair, those same strands weren't pulled back. The effect was pleasing to look at, for it gave her a softer look.

She started to unbutton her shirtwaist, and he felt his skin warm with anticipation. While they had been sharing this room for a couple of weeks, he had been in the habit of closing his eyes as soon as he got into bed. Usually, he drifted off to sleep by the time she came to bed, but there had been one or two nights when he was still awake. On those nights, he had simply kept his eyes closed so she would assume he was asleep. Doing so had avoided any potentially uncomfortable situations.

Then, in the morning, she was always dressed and ready for the day by the time he woke up. So there hadn't been a time when he'd caught her without any clothing on, and he supposed if he had, it wouldn't have been shocking. Neither one of them were virgins. They'd been married before. They were well aware of how someone of the opposite sex looked without clothes on.

A part of him missed being able to look at a woman who wasn't wearing anything. Even on nights when nothing happened, it had been nice to see Jennifer. It would be nice to see Deanne as well.

And who knew? Perhaps seeing Deanne might stir something within him that had died long ago.

She had her back turned to him, so there wasn't much to see as she removed her clothes. He had the perfect view of her backside, however. That, in itself, was lovely. He'd always thought the way a woman's body curved at the waist and at the hips was attractive. Even with clothes on, the female form appealed to him. It was much more so when the clothes were off. And Deanne had a very nice shape to her.

The mirror was in front of her. Given the angle she was standing, he only got a glimpse of one of her breasts. In a way, it was far more intriguing since he couldn't see the whole thing.

He waited for a sign that old desires could be revived, but he wasn't even getting slightly erect. Disappointed, he settled onto his back and let out a long sigh. Well, he had told her there would be nothing going on between them in bed. At least he hadn't given her any false expectations.

He closed his eyes. He heard her shuffling around and figured she was putting on her nightgown. Soon after, the light from the kerosene lamp went out and she got into the bed next to him. The bed wasn't that big, so they couldn't help but touch at some point. He was in the habit of sleeping on his back, and she tended to roll up on her side, facing away from him. So that tended to leave his arm pressed against her back unless he folded his arms over his chest.

On this night, he opted to let his arm remain settled down at his side. If nothing else, it was nice to have the physical contact with her. He could at least enjoy doing simple things like touching her back. Or her hand. Just because he couldn't make love to her, it didn't mean he had to forget everything that was enjoyable in a marriage.

Feeling better, he relaxed and let himself drift off to sleep.

Chapter Thirteen

DEANNE SORTED THROUGH the packages of jerky in the barrel close to the window. She was quickly learning that Tanner Bloom was a picky customer. He had to have everything a particular way. She secretly felt sorry for his wife. It was no wonder his wife refused to do the shopping.

"Make sure the package is nice and smooth. I don't want any curled edges," Tanner said.

"I'm checking everything carefully," Deanne assured him as she continued her search for the perfect jerky package.

She made a mental note to be more careful when putting a new shipment of items on the shelves or in the barrels. One never knew when someone like Tanner would come into the store.

When she finally found what she was looking for, she pulled it out and showed it to him. "What do you think?"

He took it and turned it over. After a few seconds of studying it, he nodded. "That'll do." He gave it back to her. "Add it to my order."

She nodded and carried the package to the counter. She wrote down the last of his order. Then she waited until he figured out where he wanted to put the jerky in the crate. In the end, he chose to slip it between the flour and the coffee beans.

"How much do I owe you?" he asked.

"The total comes to $2.35."

His eyebrows furrowed. "That much?"

"The man who makes the jerky raised his prices."

"When was this?"

"Three days ago." She stared at him in disbelief. How could he not have noticed the big sign she had posted above the barrel announcing the price change? He'd kept her sorting through that barrel for a good five minutes.

He shook his head but dug out the extra penny from his pocket and put it on the counter.

She resisted the urge to roll her eyes. Because he kept her busy for an entire half hour looking for all the things he wanted that met up to his expectations, she still had a lot of items to put away that had arrived that morning. She was going to have to rush through lunch in order to close the store on time. She hated closing late because it meant Marsha had to watch the children longer and keep the food warm for everyone.

Forcing a smile, she took the money from Tanner and put it into the leather pouch. Most customers were a delight to work with, but there were some who made her very happy when they left the store.

Once Tanner was gone, she went to the back room where stacks of crates were waiting for her. Bill had opened all of them and was organizing them according to type.

"It sounds like Tanner was giving you grief out there," Bill told her as she approached.

"Before today, I had no idea how a little crinkle on a package could be the source of so much distress."

He chuckled. "If you think Tanner is bad here, just imagine how he is at home."

She cringed. "I'd rather not think about what his poor wife and children go through."

"At least you only have to deal with him once in a while. Fortunately, he doesn't come in much."

"Thank goodness for small favors."

He took out the utensils that were in one of the opened crates and placed them neatly on top of a crate that hadn't been opened yet.

"While you put these out there, I'll get the cups ready," he said as he handed her the utensils.

She hurried to take them from him then put them where they belonged in the store. She hadn't thought of it before, but it was nice to work with someone who was as pleasant as Bill was. It was even better they were married. With a smile, she returned to the back room, more excited to see him than to retrieve more items to put in the main part of the store.

THAT NIGHT, BILL WATCHED Deanne undress again. He didn't feel as awkward about it as he had the previous night. Tonight, his goal wasn't to see if he could get an erection. He was simply enjoying the opportunity to get to see her without some clothes on.

This time, she did notice that he was watching her. She happened to glance in the mirror, and her gaze went to him. She gasped and spun around, clutching the nightgown to her chest.

After a moment, she let out a relieved laugh. "For a moment, I thought you were someone else. You don't usually sit up in bed that long."

She put the nightgown over her head, and he got a clear view of her nice round breasts before the gown fell down her body.

Well, that was certainly better than seeing her from the back. He cleared his throat. "I'm not tired. I thought if you weren't tired, we could talk for a while."

"Talking would be nice." She flipped her braid over her shoulder and turned the wick down on the kerosene lamp. "I'm not very tired, either. You think I would be after putting all of those things away in the store."

"Sometimes it's hard to sleep on the busiest of days."

She went to the window, parted the curtains, and then opened it. "Is that enough of a breeze?"

"Yes, it feels good."

She sat next to him then asked, "What's on your mind?"

The moonlight coming in through the window gave him a good view of her face. Once more those soft curls that refused to be confined to the braid settled against her cheeks in a way that made him think that when Adam first saw Eve, he must have thought that, of all of God's creations, there wasn't anything more beautiful than woman. He smiled. "Actually, I was thinking that you're lovely to look at."

Her eyes widened in surprise. "You were thinking that?"

"I couldn't help but think it. You are a masterpiece. No artist could render better work."

She offered a shy smile. "That's beautiful. How did you come up with that?"

He shrugged. "Right after I lost the use of my legs, Winnie and Piper brought me a lot of poetry. They love poetry. They even encouraged me to write some, but my attempts were nothing like what they expected."

"What were your attempts like?"

"Pathetic." He laughed. "I had to finally tell them that no matter what they hoped, I wasn't going to turn into a writer. I was going to continue on at the general store. Numbers are a lot easier to manage than words are."

"I don't know. I thought what you said just now was poetic to me."

"To be fair, you provide good inspiration. I'm sure if you were there when I was trying to write those poems, Winnie and Piper would have been thrilled with the results."

He couldn't be sure, but he thought she blushed as she chuckled. As it was, her gaze had lowered, an indication she was both pleased but also unsure of where things were going. He reached forward and took her hand in his. "I'm very lucky you came into the store when I was looking for a wife."

She didn't respond for a moment, and he was beginning to think he had put her in an uncomfortable position. Perhaps it might be best to wish her a good night's sleep and let this be the end of this conversation for now. Her first marriage had been different from his. Certainly, these terms of endearment weren't as natural for her as they were for him.

Just as he was ready to squeeze her hand and tell her good night, she whispered, "You're nothing like Terry, and for that I'm grateful."

He couldn't recall if she'd told him the name of her first husband before or not, but she was opening up to him, which was a good sign. "I want us to have a good marriage. You're a terrific woman. Some men don't know a good thing when they have it, but I'm smart enough to know that I struck gold when I married you."

Because it seemed like the right moment, he leaned toward her and kissed her. A spark of uncertainty swept over him. While kissing was simple enough on the surface, it marked the transition in their marriage. Once physical contact was established, there was no going back to the way things had been before. But really, he didn't want it to go back to how things were before. He wanted to move forward.

He started to deepen the kiss when he felt her stiffen. He shifted away from her to give her some space. "Would you rather I not kiss you?"

"Kissing is fine. It's just that..." She paused then sighed. "I didn't think I would have to explain this to you since you said we wouldn't consummate the marriage. But you might as well know that I can't have children. I know how important children are to men. Terry and I had plenty of arguments over my inability to conceive. I'd rather not have those arguments with you, too. When I married him, I didn't know I couldn't conceive, but after being with him for six years and him being able to have a child with the woman he had the affair with, there's no denying the truth. Everyone expects a woman to be able to have children." She turned her face away from him.

He had to think over what he should say. He didn't want to come out and tell her that as much as he wanted to consummate the marriage, he wasn't physically able to. What man would want to admit something so embarrassing? But at the moment, what he was going through faded in comparison to what she was going through. The more he heard about her past, the less he wanted to know. She'd had more problems to contend with in her first marriage than whether or not she could have children. One would never have guessed she had all of these burdens she was carrying around with her. She kept them hidden very well.

Bill put his arm around her shoulders. "A woman's value doesn't come from whether or not she can have children. Her value comes from who she is. Deanne, you're one of the loveliest women I've ever come across. There's far more to marriage than having children. There's companionship and love. A man is incomplete without the right woman in his life. I think you and I can have something wonderful. I'm sorry for what Terry put you through. If I could erase all of that for you, I would. All I can do is offer you a fresh beginning. I don't need more children. I have Amber and Vernon. And they're now your children, too. I know this is all new, and we're still getting used to each other. Right now, I only intend to kiss you. And touch your hand and maybe even hold you."

At some point, he hoped he might be able to enjoy things of a more physical nature with her, but he wasn't able to do that right now. And that being the case, there was no sense in making her think they would be doing more.

She relaxed against him, and though she hurried to brush it away, he noticed the tear that slid down her cheek.

He cupped the side of her face with his hand so that he could turn her face toward him. Then he kissed her in hopes that it might help soothe over the fears and doubts she'd brought into the marriage. This time when he went to deepen the kiss, she didn't stiffen against him.

He didn't go too far with the kiss. For now, soft and gentle seemed to be best.

He proceeded to kiss her cheek and then encouraged her to lie down next to him. Once they had the blanket brought up to their chests, he pulled her into his arms and kissed the top of her head. He didn't know how long it was before he fell asleep, but he was sure that he felt a few tears moisten his nightshirt.

Chapter Fourteen

THE NEXT MORNING WHILE Deanne got ready for the day, she did something she hadn't done in a very long time; she decided to wear her hair down. She did pull back the sides with her pins just so that it wouldn't get in her face, but other than that, it fell in soft waves down to the middle of her back. She thought of the pretty ribbons and barrettes in the general store. Maybe she'd buy a couple of them. They would be more attractive in her hair than the plain pins she was used to.

Amber came bounding into the room and gasped in surprise when she saw her. "You're wearing your hair down."

"I haven't worn it down in years."

"You're so pretty. You should wear it down all the time."

Deanne smiled at the compliment. "Thank you. You're pretty, too. And you have more curls than I do. Your hair will be nicer than mine when you grow it down your back."

"It will?"

"You're going to break many hearts when you're older. I feel sorry for the poor young men. One look at you, and they won't stand a chance."

Amber shook her head. "I'm not going to break anyone's heart. It'd be gross to take someone's heart out of their chest and smash it on the ground."

Deanne hadn't thought a simple comment like that would be taken in such a literal manner. Did children not understand what commonly used expressions really meant? By the look on Amber's face, Deanne concluded that children didn't grasp the concept of figurative speech.

She drummed her fingers on the dresser as she considered how to best explain what she meant. "I don't mean that you'll actually break a young man's heart. Um, well, when you turn into a young lady, young men will start to fall in love with you. You can only pick one to marry. That means the ones you don't marry will be sad for a while."

Amber breathed a sigh of relief. "That doesn't sound gross."

"No, it's not. You won't do anything disgusting."

"Good because that's only something boys do. Like Vernon. He used to play in muddy puddles at the farm. I had to run and drag him to the house and help Pa wash him."

Deanne's eyes grew wide. "That's a lot of work. Was this after your pa got his wheelchair?"

Amber nodded. "That's why I had to do most of the work. This house is better. Vernon doesn't run all over the place anymore."

"That is good." After working at the store all day, the last thing Deanne felt like doing was washing a child in a tub.

"Now, Vernon just gets stuck."

"Stuck?"

"I told him not to jump on his bed, but he did. And now he can't get out."

"What do you mean he can't get out?" How was it possible that someone couldn't get out of their bed? It wasn't like the mattress could open up and swallow them.

Amber waved for her to follow her, so Deanne put the pins she didn't need in the top drawer and went to the other bedroom.

As it turned out, Vernon wasn't even on the mattress. He was under it. Part of the mattress was on top of him. Deanne lifted it and saw that he had somehow managed to get stuck between two of the wooden boards that were nailed into the bedframe in order to support the mattress.

Vernon looked up at her and giggled.

Amber rolled her eyes. "He thought the muddy puddles were funny, too."

Deanne had to resist the urge to chuckle since Amber wasn't the least bit amused by the whole thing. Deanne pushed the mattress aside and reached under Vernon's arms to pull him up. She had to wiggle him in order to get him out, but in the end, he was freed and took off running out of the room.

Deanne set the mattress back in place just as Bill came up to the doorway. "What's taking everyone so long this morning?"

"Vernon got stuck under the bed," Deanne told him.

"He was jumping on the bed," Amber added. "I told him not to, but he wouldn't listen to me."

"How did he get stuck under the bed if he was jumping on top of it?" Bill asked.

Amber shrugged. "He was jumping one moment and under there the next."

"Just when I think I've been through everything you kids can do, you come up with something new," Bill said.

Once Deanne was done making the bed, she walked over to Amber who was in the doorway.

"You haven't seen me break hearts yet," Amber told her pa, "but I'll do that someday."

Bill frowned. "Break hearts?"

"It sounds gross, but it won't be." Amber turned to Deanne. "What's for breakfast?"

Startled by how quickly the girl could change a topic, it took Deanne a moment to say, "Eggs and sausage. I'm going to make those now."

"Can I crack the eggs?" Amber asked.

Since Amber enjoyed cracking eggs, Deanne indicated her agreement.

Amber ran down the hall.

Worried that Amber was going to start cracking eggs before she had a chance to make sure bits of shells wouldn't get into them, Deanne began to go after her, but a touch on her hand stopped her.

"I don't recall ever seeing you with your hair down," Bill said. "I like it."

Her face warmed with pleasure. She had hoped he would notice that she'd made an effort to look attractive for him, and judging by the way he was smiling at her, she had succeeded.

He squeezed her hand. "I hope I can focus on the ledger at work. You're going to make it hard for me to think of anything but you."

"You can always come out of the back room when I'm not busy if you want to see me," she suggested, a teasing tone she didn't usually use in her voice.

He gave her a playful smile as he let his thumb trace the top of her fingers. "Would it be wrong if I decided not to open the store today?"

Her body shivered in the most pleasant way. She had no idea that a simple touch could be so profound. Clearing her throat, she said, "I don't think the customers will be happy if you keep the store closed."

"I know you're right, but you can't blame a husband for trying, can you?"

She didn't expect to experience a moment of shyness around Bill since she'd been married before, but she was unable to maintain eye contact with him. Like last night, he was looking at her and saying things that made her feel the strangest sensations. She didn't know whether to jump up and down in excitement or run off and hide because she worried she might say or do something stupid to ruin the moment.

"At least the customers can't come here when we're at home." He kissed her hand. "I won't keep you any longer than I have."

She didn't mind that he had made her linger in the hallway longer than she intended. She hoped he might cause her to linger for a while in the future.

She heard Amber let out an "Oops" from the kitchen and knew she had to deal with whatever situation she was going to find in that room. She cleared her throat and said, "If you finish the recordkeeping earlier than you expect, it'd be nice to have you nearby."

His smile let her know that her answer made him happy.

Her heart still beating faster than normal, she hurried to the kitchen.

IT TURNED OUT TO BE an unusually busy day in the store, and Deanne was hardly able to catch her breath. Even Bill had to come out and help her. She went about the place to grab the items the customers needed while he took care of the monetary transactions.

Finally, when things calmed down, Bill was able to return to the back room. Considering the number of purchases that had been made, it was going to take him quite some time to update his ledger.

It wasn't until almost two when she realized she hadn't had lunch. She ended up resorting to putting up the sign letting people know the store was going to be closed for fifteen minutes so that she could satisfy her growling stomach.

Bill looked up from the desk where receipts were scattered all over the place. "I should have told you to keep your hair up. I had no idea that everyone was going to come in to see the prettiest woman in town."

She chuckled as she went to the shelf where she put her sandwich. "I think the sudden flow of customers is due to the fact that most people just got paid."

"I've been here for years, and I've never seen it this busy."

"It must have been this busy at some point." She glanced at him. "Did you have anything to eat yet?"

"I did. You make a good sandwich, by the way."

"Sandwiches are easy. There's nothing to making them."

She went to the desk and found a clear area to set the sandwich on. Then she retrieved a cup and poured water into it. When she realized Bill was watching her, she turned her gaze to him.

"What is it?" she asked.

"There's nothing wrong with accepting compliments when someone gives them to you."

"I accepted your compliments last night and this morning."

"Yes, that's true. So why won't you accept them now?"

She rolled her eyes and sat across from him. "Bill, there's no way half the town came in here this morning just to see me, and all I did was put some peanut butter and jam between two slices of bread."

He backed away from his side of the desk and wheeled his chair so that he was sitting next to her. At once, the most pleasant sensation spread through her entire body.

He brushed her hair over her shoulder. "If I wasn't already working here, I'd make the trip to this store just to see you."

She didn't know how to respond to that, but he spared her from having to come up with something when he cupped the side of her face and urged her to lean toward him. Heartbeat picking up, she did as he wished. As soon as his lips brushed hers, she felt the same wave of weakness come over her that had come over her last night.

Terry hadn't made it a habit of being gentle with her. With him, kissing was more of a demand, and that demand always led to him satisfying his basic needs. She hadn't realized a kiss could be this enjoyable. It was nice to be treated with such tenderness. Bill didn't have to tell her that he genuinely cared about her. She knew he did by how gentle and sweet he was being. For the first time in her life, she knew what it was like to be desired.

Bill wasn't in any hurry to stop kissing her, and quite frankly, she wasn't, either. She drew closer to him. The action seemed to encourage him, for he traced her lower lip with his tongue. It took her a moment to realize he wasn't going to just thrust his tongue into her mouth. He was asking for permission to enter her. And she was more than happy to grant it.

As he'd been up to now, he continued to be gentle with her. She had no way of knowing how long he spent kissing her, but she was very happy to be right here with him doing this. Truly, there was no other place she'd rather be.

After some time, his mouth left hers, and he left a trail of kisses down her cheek and then down her neck. She let out a contented sigh. She had no idea her skin was so sensitive. And, as it turned out, other areas on her body were responding to him, too. Her nipples hardened, and the area between her legs began to ache in a way that was unfamiliar to her. With Terry, things had been done out of the commitment she'd made to him on her wedding day, but she felt no such duty compelling her to be with Bill like this.

It was so different that she couldn't help but be surprised. She had assumed a woman wasn't supposed to get the same kind of pleasure from doing this kind of thing like a man obviously did. Even if Terry hadn't loved her, he had loved being in the bed with her.

When Bill brought his mouth back to hers, she noticed there was a hint of urgency in the way he was kissing her, but he was still mindful to be gentle with her. How could a woman not enjoy this kind of kissing? And how could a woman not want to do more when being treated so well during a private moment?

She would have continued on with him forever if possible, but she remembered she still had to eat and then return to work. Something like this was better explored further in the privacy of their bedroom.

It was with great reluctance that she pulled away from him. "I'm sorry, Bill, but more of this will have to wait. I only meant to stay here for fifteen minutes."

His eyes grew wide and he glanced at the doorway. "You don't think someone is in the store, do you?"

"No. I put the sign up saying I'd be back in fifteen minutes before I locked the door."

He let out a relieved sigh. "I know we're married, but I'd rather not have someone figure out what's going on back here." He moved the wheelchair back toward the desk and reached for the pocket watch. He blinked in surprise. "It's 2:35."

She gasped. "Already?" She took the pocket watch from him to make sure he wasn't joshing her.

"You came back here just a couple of minutes after two." He gave her a wicked grin. "I probably should feel guilty for keeping you here longer than you intended, but I don't."

Her face flushed with a mixture of shyness and excitement. She had no idea marriage could include such playfulness.

"I'll be good and let you eat." Bill paused and wheeled himself back over to her. He gave her another kiss. "Now, I'll be good."

She was sure her face was a bright red color by now since it grew even warmer from pleasure. She put his pocket watch on the desk. She didn't know if she could eat with him in the room. The way he continued to smile at her was playing havoc on her nerves.

"I think I'll take the sandwich and water out there," she said as she collected them. "I need to open the store back up."

"I'll miss you."

She laughed. "You're silly. I'll still be in the store."

"Yes, but you won't be in this room. I won't have the pleasure of talking to you."

"We didn't do a lot of talking."

"No, and that's why the time went by much too fast." He winked at her.

She had to get out of this room. Her heart was beating much too fast, and she was having the hardest time concentrating on anything but him. If she kept talking to him, he was going to render her unable to do her job. As it was, she was going to feel awkward talking to customers when she was aware that she was slick between her legs, which was a reminder of how much she'd enjoyed being back here with Bill.

She suspected she would enjoy it quite a bit if Bill were to touch her down there or, better yet, enter her. She had to remind herself that this wasn't that kind of marriage. Apparently, they were going to kiss, but Bill had said they wouldn't consummate the union.

Of course, he'd said that before they married. She wondered if that was going to change now that it was apparent they were getting along much better than she'd dreamed possible. Or, perhaps, he couldn't. He was in a wheelchair. Did that impact his ability to make love to her? She was tempted to ask, but her shyness stopped her.

She hurried to leave the room and then took down the sign from the window so that people knew the store was open again. Fortunately, someone came in within the first few minutes. That gave Deanne the distraction she most needed so she could finally calm down and think of something other than Bill.

Chapter Fifteen

THAT EVENING BILL SAT on the bed with every intention of watching Deanne undress. Since she hadn't shied away from him last night when she'd caught him watching her undress and since she'd been receptive to him in the back room of the store that day, he didn't feel quite so awkward exploring the more intimate side of their relationship.

Part of his eagerness to watch her undress was due to the fact that he'd felt a surge of warmth flood his loins while they'd been kissing, and this warmth had caused him to get somewhat hard. It wasn't enough to do anything, but it was more than what he'd thought was going to happen when he began kissing her. He wanted to know if that would happen again. Could it be that fully opening himself up to the intimate aspect of his marriage would prompt him to be able to have an erection?

At the moment, he was waiting for Deanne to come into the room. Right after she'd helped him get into the bed, Amber had called out that Vernon wouldn't stay in bed, so she had left to deal with that task. He could only make out half of what was going on in the children's bedroom, and that was only because Amber's voice was so loud that it had a tendency to carry across the house.

"She can't read a book to you," Amber said. "She needs to wake up early."

There was a pause before Bill heard Amber say, "Then I want you to read this book."

Vernon didn't seem happy about her choice since Bill heard him cry out in protest. Bill found himself chuckling despite the frustration he was sure that Deanne was experiencing. He'd had his share of evenings when he had to coax Vernon into going to bed.

Bill couldn't be sure how long Deanne read to the children, but it was completely dark out when she returned to their bedroom.

She didn't hide her surprise as she shut the door. "I thought you'd be asleep by now. I was in there for a long time."

Bill shrugged. "It wasn't that long."

"It was at least a half hour." She pulled the pins out of her hair then picked up the brush. "Do you get uncomfortable sitting up in a bed for that long? You don't have anything supporting your back."

"I'm fine."

She eyed him in a way that let him know she didn't believe him.

"I am," he insisted.

With a shrug, she brushed her hair. After a few seconds, she put the brush down and approached him. "I'd feel better if you had some support. If I sit on a bed for a long time like that, my back hurts. I'll fluff the pillow and press it up against the wall. Then you can scoot back and be more comfortable."

Maybe he should have let her do that, but another part of him—the one that had been subdued for a long time—compelled him to reach out and pull her onto his lap. She let out a startled shriek, so he brought his mouth to hers before she woke the children.

She was too shocked to do anything for a couple of seconds, but then she let out a sigh and wrapped her arms around his neck and kissed him in return. Then she proceeded to wiggle closer to him. This was a good sign. Maybe he hadn't been the only one who'd found all the kissing they'd done earlier that day arousing.

He sought her permission to enter her mouth, and she parted her lips to let him in. With a groan, he explored her mouth in earnest. He enjoyed the softer kisses. There was no way he'd ever stop doing those, but there was something about this type of kissing that brought forth the desires that had been suppressed for far too long.

Once more, the stirring of desire coursed through him, and since he was in the privacy of their bedroom, he saw no reason to hold back on giving into it, to see where it would lead. He wanted to make love to her. He wasn't sure if she had enjoyed being in bed with her first husband, but he wanted to show her that being with him would be something she could look forward to.

He brought his hand up to the top of her shirtwaist and began to undo the buttons. He made it halfway down her shirtwaist when she pulled away from him. At first, he thought she was going to remind him that he'd told her they weren't ever going to consummate their marriage, but she undid the rest of her buttons then tossed her shirtwaist and the chemise to the floor. He had only managed to glimpse her breasts last night. Being able to see them up close was much better.

He wasn't sure how far he would be able to go, but something was better than nothing, and he did miss being able to touch and explore a woman's body. He cupped one of her breasts in his hand then leaned forward to kiss the side of her neck. She let out a light moan. Encouraged, he caressed her breast, taking his time to memorize how perfect it felt in his hand. He couldn't think of anything more lovely on a woman than her breasts.

He urged Deanne to settle onto her back so he could lean toward her and better explore her. He brought his mouth to her nipple and teased it with his tongue. He recalled that being something a woman enjoyed, and as Deanne wound her fingers through his hair, he was assured he was succeeding in bringing her enjoyment. He was enjoying it, too. Not only was it of the utmost pleasure to satisfy his longing to be with her this way, but the increased hardening of his penis gave him hope that he might be able to consummate their marriage.

"Do you want me to remove my skirt?" Deanne asked, slightly out of breath as she caressed his shoulders.

He lifted his head then scooted up so he could kiss her for a wonderfully long moment. "Yes. I'd like to see all of you, if you don't mind."

Her face was already flushed with desire, but he detected her cheeks becoming a little pinker as she said, "No, I don't mind."

He shifted away from her so she could remove the skirt and undergarments. He had fun watching her. It was like unwrapping a gift. A very lovely and beautiful gift. And once she was lying naked in front of him, he was aware that he was fully erect. This was what he remembered being intimate to be like, back before he had put all of these passions and desires behind him, back when he felt like a complete man.

He traced Deanne's body with his hand, taking his time to go over her curves, noting how soft and warm she was. There was no fantasy that could compete with her.

He turned his gaze to her face and saw that her eyes were closed and her lips slightly parted. The expression on her face indicated she wanted more of this. He had every intention of doing more. Before they went to sleep, she would be fully satisfied. And, perhaps, he would be, too.

He brought his lips to her cheek and kissed her. "You make me ache to be with you," he whispered as he slid his hand between her legs.

She let out a soft moan and parted her legs, a silent invitation for him to continue what he had started. He brought his mouth to hers and slid a couple of fingers into her. She clutched his shoulders and lifted her hips to take him deeper into her. He found her sensitive nub with his thumb and began to rub it as he stroked her core with his fingers. She moaned in pleasure and dug her fingers into his skin. He lifted his head so he could watch her as he sought to intensify her pleasure.

How he'd missed this. All of it. He missed the kissing. He missed the pleasure of looking at a woman's body without clothes getting in his way. He missed feeling a woman's breasts. He missed putting his fingers into her and noting the wet heat that hinted at just how gratifying it was going to be when he entered her. Most of all, he missed the mounting tension that played out in the bed until there was no choice but to give in to release.

The moment Deanne cried out and her body grew still, he knew she'd found her release. He gently rubbed her sensitive nub, doing his best to prolong the heights of her pleasure. Once she relaxed, he brought his mouth to hers and kissed her for several long moments. Though his body was prompting him to enter her, he wanted to keep her suspended in her state of bliss for just a little longer. She was his second chance at a marriage that would fulfill every aspect of his life, and, in turn, he wanted to offer her the love and tenderness she hadn't received from her first husband.

She turned toward him and brought her hand down the nightshirt he wore. It wasn't until he felt her hand go down his chest that he realized what she was doing. He shifted so that it was easier for her to bring her hand to his erection. Even through the fabric, her touch was exquisite.

He settled onto his back and lifted his nightshirt. She got on top of him and took him into her. He groaned, clasped her thighs, and lifted his hips to go all the way into her. Yes, this was good. So very good.

He closed his eyes and gave into the need to move inside her. She worked with him, and before long, they established a rhythm that led to his eventual release. He called out her name and gave into the waves of pleasure that consumed him. It'd been so long since he'd experienced this. He'd forgotten how intense it was.

He had no way of knowing how long he was suspended in the clouds, but at long last, he drifted back to Earth. He urged her to lean toward him so he could wrap his arms around her. He kissed her for a couple of minutes before he whispered, "Thank you."

"I don't know why you're thanking me," she replied. "You're not the only one who got enjoyment from this."

"Maybe not, but it's been a long time since I felt like a whole man." He caressed her cheek. "You complete me, Deanne. I love you."

"I love you, too."

He cupped the side of her face and kissed her again.

Afterward, she got off of him, brought the blanket up around them, and settled into his arms.

He closed his eyes and let out a contented sigh. This was nice. What a difference love could make. He kissed the top of her head and drifted off to sleep.

Chapter Sixteen

DEANNE WOKE EARLY THE next morning. She was still tucked up next to Bill, and the blanket was wrapped around them both. She couldn't recall a time when she'd been more comfortable, or content. She had no idea marriage could be so wonderful.

Terry had taken her to bed many times throughout their years of marriage, but he'd never made love to her. She wouldn't have thought it possible that a woman could get such pleasure from the act. With Terry, it had been something done in hopes of conceiving a child. When she realized she wasn't able to have children, it turned into something she was obligated to do in order to fulfill her marriage vows. She'd secretly been grateful when he started to seek out another woman's bed because it meant he finally left her alone.

There had been no love in that marriage. At first, there had been a sense of companionship, but the longer she went without conceiving a child, the less inclined he was to be pleasant when he was around her.

With Bill, it was so different. Even knowing she'd never give him more children, he wanted to be with her.

She lifted her head and looked at Bill. The sunlight was starting to filter in through the window, and it gave her a perfect view of him. He was a very handsome man.

She would have spent more time watching him as he slept, but more pressing needs prompted her to get out of bed and get ready for the day. It wasn't until she was brushing her hair that Bill stirred from sleep. Her heartbeat picked up, and she hurried to put the last pin in her hair. She swept her hair over her shoulders then went over to him.

His eyes grew wide. "How late is it?"

She offered him a reassuring smile and leaned down to kiss him. "It's still early. You have plenty of time to get ready for the day. I couldn't sleep, so I got up."

"I'll make the coffee stronger this morning to help you stay awake."

"I don't mind being tired. There are worse things I could go through."

She was ready to straighten up, but he put his arms around her and urged her to kiss him again. She sighed in contentment and gave into the heady experience of being with him.

"I just wanted to enjoy this moment before the children wake up," he whispered when the kiss ended. "Once they're up, it's impossible to get any time alone."

As if to prove his point, they heard the pitter-patter of feet coming down the hall.

He chuckled and put his arm around her shoulders. "Alright, I'm ready to get out of bed."

She helped him into the wheelchair then gave him the chamber pot.

"What do you want for breakfast?" she asked.

"How about morning pie?"

She groaned. "I wish I never told Vernon that pancakes were like pie. No one is going to let me forget it."

"I happen to like them. They're my favorite breakfast item."

She heard someone leave the house and figured that had to be Vernon. She had to make sure he was going to use the outhouse instead of the front yard. "I'll be back to see if you need anything."

He waved for her to go, and she slipped out of the room, shutting the door behind her so that he had his privacy.

She hurried to the front door and stepped outside to see if Vernon had gone in this direction. She breathed a sigh of relief when she didn't see him in the front yard.

Feeling the weight of someone's gaze on her, she scanned the other houses and saw that the crotchety woman who'd complained about Vernon was watching her from her porch. The woman didn't smile or wave. She just stared at her. Hiding her annoyance, Deanne went back into the house. It was a shame one couldn't pick their neighbors.

She ran to the back door and was relieved to see Vernon coming out of the outhouse. While she could understand people not wanting to see a little boy relieve his bladder, she didn't know why they had to be so mean about it. He was just a child, after all. She was quickly learning that a lot of things children did were done out of innocence. They didn't understand concepts like modesty. It was something they had to be taught.

She waited for Vernon to come into the house before she closed the door. "Pa said he'd like morning pie this morning. What do you think?"

Before she had time to blink, he was running for the kitchen and calling out, "Morning pie! Morning pie!"

She followed him and was surprised to see his shoulders slump in despair. "What is it?"

"There's no pie."

"I haven't made it yet." Hadn't he noticed that she hadn't been cooking when he went outside? The kitchen was right on the way to the back door.

Apparently, he hadn't noticed since he asked, "Why not?"

She laughed. "Because I have to make the batter first. It's not even six thirty. Seven is when we eat breakfast."

The answer didn't seem to satisfy him, for he let out a heavy sigh.

"Let's go to your bedroom so your sister can help you get dressed. By then, I should be making morning pie. They cook fast."

"Alright."

She tried to recall if she'd been impatient as a child, but that part of her life seemed so long ago that it was hard to recall. Either children were naturally impatient or it was a part of his personality. With a shake of her head, she followed Vernon to his bedroom to wake up Amber so the children could get ready for the day.

"OF COURSE, I DON'T make it a habit of talking about other people," Velma was saying as Deanne added up the total of her bill. "I'm just not sure if Benny is the right choice for Myrtle. He might be two years older than her, but he acts like he's much younger." In a lower voice she added, "The other day, I caught him playing on the train tracks right before a train was due to arrive. Now, tell me, do you think someone like that is ready for marriage?"

To avoid answering the question, and therefore getting wrapped up in something that wasn't her business, Deanne smiled at the eighteen-year-old and said, "I'm sure Myrtle will choose a suitable man for marriage." She lifted the piece of paper that would serve as Velma's receipt. "The total will be $4.65. Do you want me to put it on your father's account?"

"Oh, no. Pa gave me the money." Velma proceeded to open her drawstring purse and take out the money.

While she counted out the money, Deanne put the items into two crates. She was done by the time Velma had put everything on the counter.

"I reported it to the person working at the train station," Velma said.

"Reported it?" Deanne asked.

"What Benny was doing."

Oh! The train tracks. Deanne had already forgotten that Velma had said he'd been playing on them.

"The station manager said he'd talk with Benny's parents," Velma continued.

Deanne's eyebrows furrowed. "His parents? But isn't he twenty-three?" She bit her tongue. It really wasn't her place to get involved in this.

Velma gave her a pointed look. "He might be twenty-three, but he acts like he's ten."

Deanne took the money, counted it, and then put it in the leather pouch. "I'll carry the second crate for you." Deanne took the crate in her arms. With a glance at the woman behind Velma, she said, "I'll be back in a moment."

Iola nodded and put the sack of flour and basket of eggs on the counter. Deanne hurried to take the crate out to the buggy. After thanking Velma for stopping by, she went back into the store.

"Thank you for your patience," Deanne told Iola and totaled up her bill.

"You know she only picks on Benny because she's upset he prefers Myrtle to her," Iola said. "She's been chasing after him for years, but he has no interest in her. When they were in school, she used to hide his things, and she'd tell the teacher every little thing he did that was wrong. It wore the poor teacher out. I know because he used to tell my husband about it. My husband is the head of the schoolboard."

Oh dear. Deanne hadn't expected to learn even more about the people in town than she wanted to know. She'd forgotten what small towns were like after living in Omaha. Her hometown was just like this. If these people were talking about Benny so much, she could only imagine what they were saying about her.

Deanne cleared her throat. "That'll be $0.23."

Iola blinked as if she had forgotten about the flour and eggs.

Deanne smiled. "I apologize if I seem rude. It's just that I need to work on the inventory list with my husband. We need to get it to Mr. Samuel before the end of the day."

Iola chuckled. "If that's your excuse for spending time in the back room with your husband, I'll pretend to believe it." She put $0.23 on the counter and winked. "I noticed how long this store was closed yesterday afternoon." She collected the flour and eggs then headed out of the store.

Deanne was glad there were no other customers in the place or they might have noticed how red her face was. Exactly what did Iola, and possibly others, think she and Bill had been doing in the back room?

Forget what they were thinking. It's what they were saying that really mattered.

Trying to push the conversation with Iola aside, she put the money into the leather pouch. Usually, she would take the lull in activity to ask Bill if there was anything he needed, but she wasn't sure if she should do that right now. She might be better off staying out here where people could see her from the windows. At least then, no one would give her knowing winks.

Bill emerged from the back room with the inventory list on a clipboard on his lap. "Is everyone gone?" he asked as he scanned the store.

"Yes, the last customer just left."

"In that case, do you want to take a break and join me in the back room?" He wiggled his eyebrows suggestively.

Her face flushed even more. "We can't."

"Why not?"

"Because..." She glanced out the windows to make sure no one was coming toward the store then walked over to him. In a whisper, she said, "Iola was just in here, and she let me know that she is aware of what we were doing in the back room yesterday."

"How can she know? She wasn't with us."

"She noticed how long the store was temporarily closed."

"The store can be closed for any reason."

"I realize that, but she figured out what we were doing."

"She told you she knows we were kissing?"

"She might as well have with the way she winked at me."

He chuckled. "So what if she assumes we were kissing? We're married. Married people are allowed to kiss."

"It's just awkward to know that she knows."

"It shouldn't be." He took her hand and squeezed it. "Think of it like this: she knows you have a husband who finds you desirable. The worst that can happen is that she'll tell everyone how much I adore you."

"I suppose it's not so bad that Iola knows we were kissing."

"It's not." He nodded to the back room. "Since no one's here, let's enjoy our time alone."

"I can't do that anymore."

"Why not?"

"Because now that I know people know what we're doing back there, it's different. I feel like they're watching us."

She could tell he was looking for a way to assure her that people weren't really going to think anything was going on in the back room, but in the end, he let out a disappointed sigh and released her hand. "It's just my luck that Iola had to say something. That woman's never been able to keep her thoughts to herself."

"We can still kiss at home."

"I realize that, but it's fun to kiss you while we're at work. What's the point in having your wife work with you if you can't kiss her during the day?"

"You didn't marry me so you could kiss me. You married me to help you with the customers. You didn't want to keep pestering Archie to do this job for you."

"Yes, but then you turned out to be much better than I expected. What am I supposed to do?" He gave her an imploring look. "I'm only human."

She was beginning to feel sorry for him when she felt something caress her behind. She gasped and swatted his hand away. "Bill, you're awful!" She giggled. "You can't do that here. I don't care how tempted you are. Someone could walk in here at any moment." She glanced at the door, and thankfully, no one was there. "We'll have plenty of time at home for this kind of thing."

"We won't be home for another five hours. You expect me to go that long without kissing you after what we did yesterday? That's not fair, Deanne. It's like you put a fancy meal in front of me, let me have a bite of it, and then tell me I can't have any more."

"One doesn't eat a fancy dinner in a store."

"No, but one can sample a piece of candy."

She groaned, but it wasn't from exasperation. He was being so sweet that she wanted to run off to the back room and kiss him like she had yesterday. Maybe it was easy for him to not worry about what other people were thinking, but it wasn't like that for her. "I don't like it when people know what I'm doing. I'd rather keep things private."

"Alright, I'll be good while we're here." He squeezed her hand. "I'll get started on the inventory list."

He released her hand and began to wheel himself over to one of the shelves.

A twinge of guilt came over her, so she followed him. "Wait." When he stopped and turned his head in her direction, she kissed him. She intended for the kiss to be short, but the truth was, she liked it so much that she let her lips linger on his for a while. "I suppose a sample now and then won't hurt."

Then, before she would be tempted to keep kissing him, and risk being caught by someone who could come into the store at any moment, she hastened to get back to work.

Chapter Seventeen

AMBER STARTED TOWARD the schoolhouse and then came running back to Deanne, Marsha, and Vernon. "How long will those kids be there?" she asked.

"They're going to be there all day," Marsha replied.

"All of them?"

"Well, yes, that's how school works," Marsha said. "You spend the day there with the others. That's why your ma put a sandwich and a treat in your pail."

"But there's so many kids. I'll get lost in there."

Deanne glanced at the children and saw there couldn't be more than fifteen of them going into the building that also served as the town hall. She supposed to a child who was used to spending the day with her brother, that would be scary. She recalled how intimidated she'd been when she first arrived in Omaha after spending her whole life in a town smaller than this one. It took her a couple of months before she got used to shopping and church.

"You've seen some of those children in church," Marsha told the girl.

"I didn't talk to any of them," Amber said. "And I wasn't alone with them."

"You won't be alone. You'll have the teacher."

When that didn't satisfy the girl, Deanne ventured, "What if you think of it like sitting in church? Pretend we're sitting around you when you're at your desk. Focus on the teacher and do what he says. Then, when you feel comfortable, take a peek at the child sitting next to you. And when you're comfortable sitting next to that child, become aware of the other child who's close to you. Before too long, you'll be comfortable with all of the children who are with you in the schoolhouse."

Amber arched an eyebrow. "Will that really work?"

"It worked for me when I was new in Omaha. I didn't have to go to school, but I did have to go out shopping around a lot of unfamiliar people."

"And you got to know them all?"

Deanne smiled as she thought of how impossible that would have been. "No, but I got comfortable being out around a lot of people, and when it came time for me to board a train to come out here to marry your pa, I wasn't scared."

"I think you should do what your ma says," Marsha said. "I can't think of a better way of handling things when you're nervous."

"And being nervous is normal," Deanne added. "Everyone in a new situation feels nervous."

"They do?" Amber asked.

Deanne nodded.

Amber glanced at the schoolhouse where the teacher was greeting the children as they went into the building. She took a deep breath then released it. "Alright. I'll pretend I'm at church."

"You'll be surprised by how quickly you'll get used to being in school," Deanne assured her.

Marsha gave the girl a pat on the shoulder before Deanne took Amber to the door of the schoolhouse. They got behind an older girl who was currently greeting the teacher. Deanne noticed the way Amber closed her eyes in an attempt to calm her racing heart and decided to give her a comforting pat on the shoulder like Marsha had done. She didn't know if it worked, but Amber opened her eyes and stepped closer to the teacher.

After the girl in front of them went into the building, the teacher turned his attention to them and smiled. "I see we have a new face this year. I'm Mr. Weebly."

"I'm Mrs. Harvey," Deanne said. "This is Amber. She's my daughter." That felt strange to say, but it was true. Even if she hadn't given birth to the girl, she was raising her. That meant she was her mother. Just as she was Vernon's mother. Even though she'd been taking care of them for the past couple of months, it didn't seem real until that moment.

Mr. Weebly turned his gaze to Amber. "I'm very happy to see you, Amber. I think you're going to enjoy being in school."

"I hope so, Preacher Daniel," Amber said then ran into the schoolhouse, keeping her gaze directly in front of her as she did so.

Mr. Weebly's eyes widened.

"I'm afraid that's my fault," Deanne hurried to explain. "She's nervous about today. I told her to pretend she was going to church. I didn't tell her to think of you as the preacher, but apparently, she took it that way."

Thankfully, Mr. Weebly understood since he offered her a smile. "All children are nervous when they first attend school. It's never failed in the twelve years I've been doing this. But don't you worry. In a few days, she'll forget all about why she was nervous. Children adapt quickly to new situations."

They did? Well, that was good news. Deanne was beginning to feel nervous on Amber's behalf, though she hadn't realized it until she saw the way the girl bolted into the schoolhouse as if something was chasing after her.

"Do you know when school ends for the day?" Mr. Weebly asked.

"Two?"

He nodded. "I let the little ones out earlier than the older ones. Those twelve and older get out at three. You can't expect a young child to sit too long in a chair."

You couldn't? Just when Deanne was getting comfortable with being a mother, she found out there was more she had to learn. It was a bit overwhelming at times. Working at the store was much easier.

Deanne said goodbye then went back to Marsha. Vernon had gotten impatient and was now running circles around the woman.

"Amber will be done with school at two," Deanne said.

"I was sure it was two. It's good to know my memory hasn't failed me." Marsha took Vernon's hand, and the three walked down the path that would take Deanne to the store. "I'll be there when she gets out. I expect she'll walk herself to and from school by next week."

"Want to go to school," Vernon said.

"You're too young to go there this year," Marsha told him. "You'll get your chance when you're seven."

After a moment of silence, Deanne asked, "Marsha, how long does it take to learn everything you need to know about children?"

Marsha chuckled. "Oh, you never stop learning. Just when you think you've figured them out, they do something new that surprises you."

"They do?"

"I'm afraid so. Each one is different. That's why you never stop learning." She gave Deanne a sympathetic smile. "You're doing fine. Being a mother isn't about what you know. It's about the care and concern you have for the child. It's not something that can be taught. It's something that has to be experienced. Just take it one day at a time. Everything will work out in the end."

Deanne relaxed. When Marsha put it like that, being a mother didn't sound so scary. "And I have you, Bill, and Henry to help me."

"You most certainly do. You don't have to go through this alone. We'll be with you every step of the way."

"Thanks. I feel much better."

"I'm glad. And I think it meant a lot to Amber that you went up to the teacher with her. That's the kind of thing a mother does, and children remember that long into the future." Marsha hugged her. "I'm going to take Vernon home. You go on and help your husband at the store."

Deanne offered a nod, wished Vernon a good day, and parted ways so she could go to the general store.

It turned out a couple of customers were already there. Noting that Bill was taking care of a man who was purchasing some items, she went over to Winnie and Piper who were struggling to reach one of the pots from a high shelf.

"Let me get a chair from the back room so I can get that for you," Deanne told them.

Winnie stopped her before she could go to the room. "We heard that Amber started school today."

Deanne glanced at the other two customers in the store who hadn't been helped yet. Since they were sorting through the sewing supplies, she supposed she had a moment to talk. "Yes," she said. "She was a bit nervous."

"That's to be expected. Piper, do you remember when we went to school for the first time?"

Piper gave a wistful smile. "Our family just arrived in this town. I was six and Winnie was eight back then. It's hard to believe it was that long ago."

"It wasn't that long ago."

"We got gray hair."

"That's just early gray. It doesn't have anything to do with our age," Winnie insisted. "Piper! Remember the dog that used to follow you to school each day. He'd stay by the schoolhouse all through the day until you were ready to go home."

"I remember him. Sometimes I miss Otis. He was such a good dog. Faithful to the very end."

"Curt didn't think too much of him. He was terrified of dogs."

Piper giggled. "I forgot all about Curt! He refused to leave the schoolhouse until I left with Otis. It wouldn't have been so strange if he hadn't been five years older than me. Can you imagine a boy that old being scared of a harmless dog?"

"Curt didn't like any kind of animal. That's just how he was."

Assuming they were going to continue reminiscing, Deanne made a move to go to the back room when Winnie put her hand on her arm. "Curt wasn't meant for small town life. When he grew up, he went to a big city. Last I heard, he works in an office somewhere."

"I think he went to Philadelphia," Piper said.

Winnie's eyebrows furrowed. "Was it Philadelphia, or was it Pittsburg?"

"I'm pretty sure it was Philadelphia."

"That doesn't sound right. I don't recall his sister saying he went to a city that ended in an 'a.'"

"What does it matter? It was somewhere in Pennsylvania."

"I suppose it doesn't matter. I just don't want my memory to start failing me." Winnie glanced at Deanne. "It's important for a woman my age to keep a sharp mind. It's why I stay active."

Piper snickered. "So you do admit you're old."

Winnie gasped. "I admit nothing of the sort. I meant that I'm keeping a sharp mind now so that it'll be easier for me to do so when I get old."

"Of course."

"It's true." When it was obvious that her friend didn't believe her, Winnie turned her attention back to Deanne. "You think I'm still young, don't you?"

"It's not fair to put her in the middle of this," Piper argued. "You're forcing her to tell you something you want to hear. We don't need to put her in such an uncomfortable position. You came here for oregano and thyme, and I came here for a new pot. The least we can do is let her get the chair."

Since Winnie let go of Deanne's arm, Deanne took that as permission to get the chair. After she got the pot and scooped out the amount of oregano and thyme Winnie wanted, all of the other customers had left.

"How are you two doing today?" Bill asked the women.

Deanne glanced at him but kept quiet as she took the payment from Winnie. Did he really want them to stay here for another half hour? Already, another customer was entering the store, and, if she was right, another one was coming in behind him. This was turning into a busy morning.

As they talked to Bill, Deanne went to help the other customers. She had no idea what time they finally left, but she and Bill had a steady stream of customers for the rest of the morning. She was never so happy to see the last customer leave.

Bill chuckled as she turned the sign on the door letting everyone know the store was going to be closed for fifteen minutes. "I'd think you wanted to go into the back room with me if you weren't so frazzled."

"It's like everyone in town decided they needed to shop today," she said, not hiding the fact that she was overwhelmed from her voice. "And it's not even a day when they all got paid."

"Now you can appreciate why I wanted to get married again. Poor Archie couldn't keep up with everyone like you can."

"I barely kept up with them."

"You were great."

She went to the back room so she could sit down for a few minutes. She closed her eyes and slowly released her breath to help herself relax.

"I know it's harder for you to go through all of that since you have to run around and grab things for people," Bill said. "But you really did handle everything well. Poor Archie used to get flustered and need to come back here for a minute to compose himself before he was ready to keep helping people. I ended up asking a couple of the customers to grab things off the shelves for other customers to keep up with it all. Though the customers didn't seem to mind, I'm relieved that I didn't have to do that today."

She opened her eyes and saw that he had pulled the wheelchair up to her chair. "I wouldn't mind it so much if this wasn't the same morning Amber started her schooling. I came here late. I'm sure that put us behind."

"Things were quiet in here until about fifteen minutes before you showed up. It wasn't busy the whole time you were gone." He took her hand in his. "I hope you don't get discouraged."

"I'm not discouraged. I'm just resting."

"Good. I think Archie would leave town if I asked him to come back to help me."

She chuckled at his joke. "I'm not going to stop working here. I like the job. It's nice to have a purpose."

"Your purpose goes beyond that of working here, but I admit it's been a big relief to have your help."

Her skin warmed in pleasure at his words.

"How did things go with Amber? Was she nervous?" he asked.

She nodded. "She was reluctant to go into the schoolhouse. I feel a bit nervous for her. I know what it's like to have to go somewhere new all by yourself. It's not easy."

"She'll get through it. We all do. She's at the age where it'll be good for her to meet other children. Aunt Marsha was right. This will be good for her."

Considering how good it was for Deanne to leave her hometown to explore the unknown, she suspected he was right. Sometimes a person had to embrace something new in order to improve their life.

"You're good with the children, Deanne," Bill told her. "I couldn't have married a better woman." He gave her a kiss.

She smiled and returned his kiss.

Chapter Eighteen

WHEN IT WAS TWO, DEANNE couldn't help but wonder how Amber's day had gone. She tried to concentrate on her work, but she kept checking the time.

The whole day had been such an unusual one. That morning, it'd been so busy she'd needed to temporarily close the store. And now time was passing so slowly because there weren't any customers. She couldn't help but note the irony. Why couldn't it be busy right now so she'd be distracted from glancing at the pocket watch all the time?

Bill must have noticed her impatience, for he suggested, "Why don't you go to Aunt Marsha's? I'll close the store by myself today."

"You don't mind?" she asked.

"If it gets busy, I'll send someone to get you."

"Alright. It's a deal." She gave him a kiss then left the store.

She had to stop herself from running to Marsha's home. There was no sense in making others wonder why she was in a hurry.

She didn't realize how important it was to her that Amber had a good day until she overheard Amber discussing her day with Marsha from the kitchen.

"Mama," Vernon called out to her from the corner of the parlor where he was playing with his toys.

It took Deanne a moment to realize he was talking to her, and the only reason she had figured that out was because he was heading in her direction with his arms raised up in a way that let her know he wanted her to pick him up.

She went over to him and gathered him into her arms. He rested his head on her shoulder, and her heart warmed. This was nice. She never thought she'd get a chance to hold a child like this. The fact that he felt comfortable enough with her to call her his mother and rest his head on her shoulder brought tears to her eyes.

"I thought I heard Vernon call out to someone," Marsha said as she came into the parlor.

Amber followed close behind, and Deanne noticed the big smile on the girl's face. Deanne relaxed. Good. The day had been a good one.

"Betty said she likes my hair," Amber said as she came up to her.

"Betty?" Deanne asked as her mind went to all of the customers she'd come across in the store.

"She's a nine-year-old student at the school," Marsha said. "While the children were playing, she came up to Amber and started talking to her. I got a chance to see her as she and Amber were leaving the schoolhouse together. It seems like Amber's made her first friend."

"Betty wants me to teach her how to decorate her hair with ribbons like this," Amber told Deanne. "Can you teach me so I can teach her?"

"I'll be happy to," Deanne replied.

Amber's grin widened. "Oh good! I told her I'm going to grow my hair all the way down to the middle of my back like yours. Then I'll be pretty like you."

"You're already pretty," Deanne said.

"But I'll be prettier when my hair is longer."

Amber spoke in such a matter-of-fact way that both Deanne and Marsha laughed.

"I'm afraid keeping her hair just past her shoulders was my idea," Marsha said. "I don't have the patience to comb through tangles. I'm glad you do."

"I braid the hair. Then it doesn't tangle so much," Deanne replied. Turning her attention back to the girl, she added, "I'm glad you had a good day. Does this mean you feel better about going to school tomorrow?"

Amber nodded. "I'm not scared anymore. Pretending I was in church worked."

Deanne smiled in pleasure that her advice had been beneficial.

"Amber and I are making cookies to celebrate," Marsha told Deanne. "I think the first batch is about ready."

Vernon perked up and wiggled to get out of Deanne's arms. "I want cookies!"

Deanne set him down, and he bolted straight for the kitchen.

"I don't know a single child who doesn't like cookies," Marsha said.

Deanne imagined there wasn't an adult who didn't like cookies, either, but there was no doubt children were more expressive in how much they enjoyed them. And that was nice. One thing she was learning about children was that they didn't hide what they thought. They were open and honest. Maybe they were open and honest to a fault at times, but she liked knowing what Amber and Vernon were thinking. It helped her to know if what she was doing as a mother was good or not.

Amber took Deanne's hand and led her to the kitchen. "I made one of the cookies for you."

"You did?" Deanne asked.

Amber nodded as they entered the kitchen. "It's in the shape of a heart. Aunt Marsha said that's the shape that means you like someone."

Marsha leaned to Deanne and whispered. "It doesn't look like a heart, but that's what it's supposed to be."

Deanne smiled. "I'm touched, Amber. I don't know what to say."

Marsha took the tray out of the oven and put it on the table so the cookies could cool off. "This is the one for you."

As Marsha had warned, the cookie was more in the shape of an awkward egg than a heart, but Deanne thought it was the best-looking cookie she'd ever seen. It was a shame she had to eat it.

"Thank you, Amber," Deanne said and hugged the girl. "It's perfect."

Amber beamed.

Marsha winked at Deanne as she helped Vernon into a chair, and Deanne turned her attention to taking the cookies off of the tray and putting them on a plate.

BILL ENDED UP CLOSING the store by himself. As he reached the front door of his aunt and uncle's house, he heard laughter coming from inside. He was ready to open the door when his uncle called out that he would get it for him.

"I heard it was unusually busy this morning at the store," Uncle Henry told him as he came up behind him on the ramp.

Bill turned his gaze to him. "Yes, but Deanne and I managed through it."

"Good to hear. I know those days used to be hard on you. Looking at you now, I can see you managed just fine. She's turned into a huge help in the store."

"Yes, she has. She's exactly what I was looking for when I posted the ad."

His uncle gave him a pat on the shoulder. "I'm glad to hear it."

"She's good with the children, too," Bill added. "She didn't stop worrying about Amber all day. She has a natural mothering instinct in her."

"Some women are like that. Deanne has a big heart. Someone like that should be a wife and mother."

Bill couldn't agree more.

Uncle Henry opened the door and helped Bill through the doorway.

Amber ran out of the kitchen and went straight over to Bill and hopped onto his lap. "I had a wonderful day. I love school!"

He hugged her. "Good. Your ma and I wondered how things went. She worried about you. She said you were nervous."

"I was, but I'm not anymore. I can't wait to go back tomorrow. Do you want to hear what happened?"

"I do. What do you think, Uncle Henry?"

"I'm ready to hear all about your day, Amber." Uncle Henry took Bill's hat and placed it next to his hat by the door. Then he picked her up. "You can tell us all about it during supper."

Bill followed them and saw the flurry of activity in the kitchen as Deanne, Aunt Marsha, and Vernon were getting the table ready. Upon noticing him, Deanne hurried over to him.

"I didn't realize it was so late," she said. "Did things get busy at the store?"

"No. It was quiet." He squeezed her hand and smiled. "You have nothing to worry about. Everything is fine."

She returned his smile. "I'll be able to help you out for the whole day tomorrow. I promise."

"Aunt Marsha and I made cookies," Amber said as Uncle Henry put her in a chair. "But you can't eat any until after the meal."

Deanne rolled her eyes. "She says that even though the rest of us snuck in a couple while making supper," she whispered.

"There's a benefit to being the cook," Bill said. "You get to sample the food."

Deanne chuckled. "That's true."

"Come on and sit," Aunt Marsha called out. "We don't want the food to get cold."

With a smile, Bill joined Deanne and went to the table where everyone had an enjoyable meal as Amber told them all about her day.

Epilogue

Deanne chuckled as Amber shifted in the chair. "You need to keep still if you want me to put these flower petals in your hair. You do want petals in your hair for the ceremony, don't you?"

The twenty-one-year-old bride finally stopped squirming. "I'm sorry, Ma. Yes, I want them. They'll make me beautiful."

"All they're going to do is enhance the beauty that's already there. Sean is a lucky man."

It was to her and Bill's benefit that they worked at the general store. Everyone in town ended up stopping by the store at some point, and she'd had plenty of opportunities to watch Sean. Not that he was aware she'd been watching him. She'd been careful to be discreet. But as soon as he came to Bill and expressed an interest in courting Amber, Deanne couldn't help but pay attention to the way he behaved. There were always clues people left without realizing it. Having dealt with her family and Terry, she'd learned the things to watch for. Fortunately, Sean was so much like Bill that she was assured he would be a good husband to Amber.

"I could barely sleep last night," Amber said. "Is that normal?"

Deanne pinned a pink rose petal into her hair. "Very normal. Today is a big day. You're going to become a wife. Everything is going to be different." She glanced at Amber's reflection in the mirror and smiled. "It's going to be an adventure. The right man can do wonders for you. I'm excited for you." Noting the way the young woman had trouble staying still, she added, "I only have five more petals to put in your hair.

After that, you can run down the aisle to greet the bridegroom at the altar."

"Oh, I can't do that! I don't want everyone to know how anxious I am. It's a secret just between us."

"My lips are sealed."

Deanne finished putting the petals into her hair then urged her to stand up so that she could make sure all of the buttons were fastened on the wedding gown. Afterward, she handed Amber the bouquet they had spent the better part of yesterday making. Then she collected the bouquets she and Amber had made for the others in the wedding party. Amber's dearest friend, Betty, was the matron of honor, and the other friends Amber had made at the schoolhouse over the years were the bridesmaids.

"You look perfect," Deanne said. "Let me tell everyone you're ready. Stay here until I come back for you."

"Don't take too long."

"I won't."

Deanne left the small room behind the altar. From the looks of it, most of the people were already assembled in the sanctuary. The preacher stood at the front with Sean.

Seventeen-year-old Vernon was near one of the pews with Fred and Calvin. Those three had become good friends over the years. Pete and Ada had three other children, in addition to Fred, and the whole family was in attendance. Likewise, Archie was there with his daughter Maybell and her husband, Jack. Calvin was their oldest, and he had two younger sisters. There were others who had come for the happy occasion. It was a full church, and thanks to Marsha, Ada, and Maybell, Deanne had been able to decorate the entire sanctuary before most of the people arrived.

Deanne went to the preacher and let him and Sean know that Amber was ready. Then she went to the entryway of the church and gave Betty and the bridesmaids their bouquets.

Bill, who'd been talking to Archie, turned to her. "Is Amber ready?"

Deanne nodded. "We better get this wedding started because she can't wait any longer."

Archie grinned. "I can say the same for the groom. He's been back here a couple of times to ask if she's ready."

"Smart men know they're getting something good when they marry." Bill gave Deanne a wink.

"I'll go find my seat." Archie shook Bill's hand then gave Deanne a hug. "Congratulations to you both."

As the groomsmen started to line up with Amber's friends, Deanne returned to the sanctuary. She went over to the organ and told Piper, "I'll wave from the foyer when everyone is ready to go down the aisle."

Piper indicated she'd watch for her signal before playing the wedding music.

By the time she returned to the back room, Amber was pacing back and forth impatiently. Deanne resisted the urge to tease her about the virtue of patience. Instead, she led Amber outside the back of the church and collected the bottom of her wedding gown so it wouldn't get dirty as they made their way to the front of the church.

Once they arrived in the entryway, Deanne hurried to urge Amber away from the doorway so that Sean wouldn't see her. "No need for the groom to see you until you're ready to walk down the aisle with your pa."

Amber chuckled then whispered, "You're so formal about this whole thing, which is surprising since you and Pa met at the train station before he took you to the preacher's house to get married."

"That was different. We didn't marry because we were in love. We married because it benefited us both," Deanne whispered back.

Amber rolled her eyes. "It quickly turned into love. I've seen all the kissing you two have done over the years."

"Sometimes love comes when you least expect it. I've been very blessed to have your pa, you, and your brother in my life. Adding a son-in-law will make the family better. Now, remember not to go down the aisle until Piper starts the 'Bridal Chorus.'"

"You've told me this five times already," Amber said.

"Have I?" Deanne asked in surprise.

Amber laughed. "Yes. And don't worry; I won't go down the aisle without Pa."

"You can't blame your ma for being excited," Bill said. "She's glad she got to help you with this day. It won't be the same when Vernon marries. Everyone knows the real attraction of the wedding is the bride."

Amber offered Deanne a smile and hugged her. "You're a good mother. I just think it's funny you worry so much."

"It's in a mother's nature to worry," Bill said. "If you have children, you'll understand."

"Thank you, Bill," Deanne leaned down to kiss him. "I better tell Piper everyone's ready."

She went to the doorway and waited for Piper to look in her direction before giving her the signal that everyone was ready. Then she hurried down the aisle and slipped into the pew next to Vernon, Marsha, and Henry.

"They're all ready," she whispered to them. Then, with a look at Vernon, she added, "Someday, you'll be at the altar waiting to get married."

"After seeing all of this fuss, I might just elope," he said.

"But this is pretty," she replied in surprise. "Don't you like the way everything looks?"

"All I see is a bunch of flowers and people in fancy clothes."

"That's part of the fun. Besides, we'll have a potluck after this. Don't tell me you aren't looking forward to the fried chicken Winnie makes."

"The potluck will be fun."

Marsha and Henry chuckled.

Deanne supposed that he was still a bit too young to appreciate the festive nature of weddings. Though he had a couple instances of infatuations with some of the girls in town, he had yet to be serious about courting any of them. But Deanne knew that before long, he'd get serious about one of them. And given how quickly Amber had grown up, he'd be a groom much too soon.

When Piper began playing the music for the bridal party, Deanne turned her attention to the front of the church. Then, when Piper played the 'Bridal Chorus', she joined everyone else in rising to their feet. And Deanne couldn't help but think that few things in this world were finer than a wedding.

Don't miss out!

Visit the website below and you can sign up to receive emails whenever Ruth Ann Nordin publishes a new book. There's no charge and no obligation.

https://books2read.com/r/B-A-MDLI-ZSCPB

BOOKS 2 READ

Connecting independent readers to independent writers.

Did you love *Interview for a Wife*? Then you should read *Eye of the Beholder* by Ruth Ann Nordin!

Mary Peters despairs that she will never marry. At nineteen, she has no prospects of finding a husband, so she takes matters into her own hands and becomes a mail-order bride. When she arrives to Omaha, Nebraska to meet the man she's due to marry, he takes one look at her homely appearance and rejects her. But fate has other plans for Mary. Dave Larson happens to be nearby and thinks she will make a good wife. Though she is stunned that someone as handsome and as kind as Dave would ask her to marry him, she accepts. She knows that this marriage will not bear the fruits of love. Love, after all, is for beautiful women. Isn't it?

Read more at https://ruthannnordinauthorblog.com/.

Also by Ruth Ann Nordin

Chance at Love Series
The Convenient Mail Order Bride
The Mistaken Mail Order Bride
The Accidental Mail Order Bride
The Bargain Mail Order Bride

Husbands for the Larson Sisters Series
Nelly's Mail Order Husband
Perfectly Matched
Suitable for Marriage
Daisy's Prince Charming

Marriage by Arrangement Series
His Wicked Lady
Her Devilish Marquess
The Earl's Wallflower Bride

Marriage by Bargain Series

The Viscount's Runaway Bride
The Rake's Vow
Taming the Viscountess
If It Takes a Scandal

Marriage by Deceit Series
The Earl's Secret Bargain
Love Lessons With the Duke
Ruined by the Earl
The Earl's Stolen Bride

Marriage by Design Series
Breaking the Rules
Nobody's Fool

Marriage by Fairytale Series
The Marriage Contract
One Enchanted Evening
The Wedding Pact
Fairest of Them All
The Duke's Secluded Bride

Marriage by Fate Series
The Reclusive Earl
Married In Haste
Make Believe Bride

The Perfect Duke
Kidnapping the Viscount

Marriage by Necessity Series
A Perilous Marriage
The Cursed Earl

Marriage by Obligation Series
Secret Admirer

Marriage by Scandal Series
The Earl's Inconvenient Wife

Misled Mail Order Brides Series
The Bride Price
The Rejected Groom
The Perfect Wife
The Imperfect Husband

Nebraska Prairie Series
The Purchased Bride
The Bride's Choice
Interview for a Wife

Nebraska Series
Her Heart's Desire
A Bride for Tom
A Husband for Margaret
Eye of the Beholder
The Wrong Husband
Shotgun Groom
To Have and To Hold
His Redeeming Bride
Forever Yours
Isaac's Decision

Pioneer Series
Wagon Trail Bride
The Marriage Agreement
Groom for Hire
Forced Into Marriage

Wyoming Series
The Outlaw's Bride
The Rancher's Bride
The Fugitive's Bride
The Loner's Bride

Standalone
A Deceptive Wager

An Earl In Time
Her Counterfeit Husband

Watch for more at https://ruthannnordinauthorblog.com/.

About the Author

Ruth Ann Nordin has written over 100 books, most of them being Regencies and historical western romances. As fun as writing is, she has also learned that time with family and friends is just as important. She has also learned that writing for passion is the best reason to write since it is what sustains an author's work for the long haul. That's why she's been able to keep writing for as long as she had. It's hard to believe she started out in ebooks back in 2009. How time flies.

Read more at https://ruthannnordinauthorblog.com/.